Diane Janes

Admiration for Diane Janis'
Voices in the Dark

"Every child should have this book! Diane Janis speaks to the heart of children using imagination and a unique and entertaining approach to environmental awareness."

Mark Victor Hansen
Co-creator, #1 *New York Times* best selling series
Chicken Soup for the Soul®
Co-author, *The One Minute Millionaire*

"*Voices in the Dark* combines Diane Janis' enthusiasm for science, astronomy, and the environment with a superb science mystery. Young readers will benefit from her years of classroom teaching. She presents many interesting facts about the sun's family of planets along with more general science concepts. While some readers will enjoy the story's scientific information, others will be drawn into the human interest drama as Erica confronts the accident that has left her blind and moves forward to overcome its limitations."

Dr. Ed Strother, Ph.D. in Experimental Physics,
Astronomer and Space Scientist for NASA and USAF

"The best books are those that weave entertainment and education into a compelling read. Diane Janis has accomplished just that with this outstanding book. Kids will love her story and wonderful illustrations of the solar system!"

Bill O'Shea
Author, *A Christmas Present*

"Diane Janis writes to entertain and inform, successfully transporting science and fantasy into an inspiring children's novel with exemplary compassion for earth."

Scott A. Herber
M.S. Senior Scientist, **Wildlife Institute and Rehabilitation Center**

"Presenting a creative approach to the wonder of science with a compassionate perspective on physical disability is a tall order. Diane Janis' *Voices in the Dark* balances both admirably. What a delightful, intriguing, and educational narrative."

Fontaine Wallace
Instructor, **Florida Institute of Technology**

"With heart, soul and appreciation for earth, Diane Janis writes a fascinating tale for children of all ages."

Carol Fuery
Author, *The Classroom Survival Series*

EARTH'S SECRET
BOOK ØNE

Voices in the Dark

Diane Janis

Prosperous Future, Inc.

Voices in the Dark
is a fictional story that teaches
science through fantasy literature.

ISBN 0-9746258-0-9

Printed in Canada

*Dedicated to the
memory of my grandparents
~ Nellie and Elmore East ~
Their unconditional love during
my childhood strengthened my
spirit for a lifetime.*

* * *

Thank you to my parents and brother for their kind support, and to Diane Lee Janowsky for her genuine encouragement.

Many thanks to my three children, April, Jacob and Trillium, for contributing their own imaginative ideas to the development of *Earth's Secret*, and to all of my students over the years whose enthusiasm for creative writing inspired my passion for this series.

Special thanks to Ailada Treerattrakoon, Pratik Patel, and Nicole Hoier from the Applied Computing Center at the *Florida Institute of Technology* for their technical assistance; to Jennifer Sword for graphic assistance; and to Dan Poynter for publication advice.

I would also like to express my personal gratitude to Ed Hensel from *Prosperous Future, Inc.* for making publication of this novel possible.

~ CONTENTS ~

Voices in the Dark

~ Chapter 1 ~

RAIN

LIKE the first warm drops of a gentle summer rain, tears began to fall from Erica's eyes. She was afraid, lonely, and desperately missed the life she had to leave behind when the hospital became her new home.

Erica wanted to go for a bike ride with Valen or go hiking with Mark. She even missed her little brother, Matthew, who always seemed to be just where Erica did not want him to be. The more she thought about how much her life had changed since the accident, the more Erica felt sorry for herself.

And what about MOON? Were Mark and Valen taking care of him the way she would? Were they giving him treats, taking him for walks, and brushing him every day? Even if they were, Erica knew Moon must be lonely without her because he had always been a loyal German shepherd.

Moon would follow Erica *everywhere*. He would even stay with her while she slept. Every night Moon would be there, watching over Erica as she drifted into peaceful dreams . . . proudly guarding her through the night.

The last thing Erica remembered seeing every night was faithful Moon. If only she could see him now . . . hug him . . . pet his smooth fur before falling asleep, it would make her feel so much better.

Unfortunately, that was not about to happen. Even if the hospital allowed dogs to visit patients, Erica would not be able to see Moon before she fell asleep. In fact, Erica would not be able to *see* anything at all because she is *blind!*

Sorrowful thoughts swam around in Erica's brain like Matthew's little goldfish in the glass bowl on his dresser. The accident wildly flashed through her mind again.

. . . *It wasn't Moon's fault! We were just having FUN. . . . I was running through the forest and I stumbled over tree roots. Moon was running right behind me really FAST, and then he banged into me! . . . I fell and hit my head on a big rock!. . . It WASN'T Moon's fault!* she thought gloomily.

~ MOON ~

The possibility that Erica's parents might blame Moon for the accident was breaking her heart. She was terribly afraid Moon would be gone when she got home.

Erica quietly whimpered to herself, "It *wasn't* his fault! It just wasn't his fault!"

She wished Mark never saw what happened in the forest that terrible day. He had promised her that he would *not* tell anyone. Erica did not want her parents to know that Moon had knocked her over. She was certain they would think her big dog was responsible for the accident and not let her have him for a pet anymore.

Furthermore, she never went to the observatory with her uncle that night. Erica was convinced that she would have been able to go to the observatory if Mark had kept the secret about her accident as he promised he would. Sure, her head hurt that night, but she had not lost her sight yet. It would have been dark, and she would have worn a hat. No one would have noticed the big bump on her head. . . . What harm was there in that?

After all, Erica had waited three years to visit the observatory and get a closer view of Saturn's rings and Jupiter's moons. It had been a very important dream ever since she first learned about the planets and looked through her uncle's telescope.

Nevertheless, what was supposed to be a dream come true had turned into a haunting nightmare. Erica was afraid that she would never have another chance to visit the observatory, and feared that her beloved Moon would never be by her side again. . . . Wilting down under the covers, she miserably sank her head into the stiff hospital pillow.

Could it get any worse? Erica certainly did not think so. However, as she sat in her hospital bed crying and brooding over all the problems the "intrusive" rock had caused, she remembered that Uncle Garwin had not come to visit her yet. Her favorite uncle, the awesome astronomy professor, **Gary William Terrano**, had deserted her. She was sure he had taken Mark, Valen, and Matthew to the observatory and completely forgotten about her!

It was all too much for Erica to endure. Her tears finally burst into a torrential rainfall, and she sobbed her heart out.

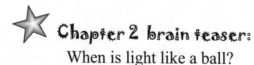 Chapter 2 brain teaser:
When is light like a ball?

Answers to brain teasers can be found on the KIDS page at *www.EarthsSecret.com*.

~ Chapter 2 ~

A SOLAR ECLIPSE

"*ARE* you okay?"

She knew the voice. Erica quickly wiped her face across the pillow to hide her tears, but she was sobbing so hard she could not speak.

"Hey, Pumpkin, what's wrong?" asked Uncle Garwin.

As tears continued to dribble from her soft brown eyes, Erica covered her face with her hands. On top of everything else, she was very embarrassed. Erica did not want her uncle to see her crying. She wanted him to think she was brave, but her hands could not silence the words that sputtered their way through her sobs.

"I d-don't want to b-b-be b-b-blind! I d-don't want to b-b-be here any-m-m-more! I want to g-go home!" she cried miserably.

"I am sure you will go home soon," assured Uncle Garwin as he gave his niece a comforting hug. "I just talked to your doctor, and he said the swelling in your brain is decreasing a little bit more every day. He thinks you will be able to leave the hospital in a few days."

Erica exploded with disappointment.

"BUT I WANT TO GO HOME NOW!" she blurted out loudly.

"I know this has been very difficult for you, Erica. You've had to endure a multitude of changes that have caused you to be afraid, and I think you have been *very* brave."

"BRAVE!" exclaimed Erica. "But I can't stop crying!"

"It's okay. Crying doesn't mean you're not *brave*," replied Uncle Garwin in a calm manner.

"It doesn't?"

"No, it doesn't. . . . Being brave means you do what you need to do even if you are afraid," he explained.

"It does?" Erica sniveled.

"Yes, and you have been *extremely* brave. Your parents told me about the medical testing the doctors have been performing since you got here. The testing alone is tough enough to go through, but you have also had to endure losing your sight. I am sure *that* could even make a superhero cry!"

For the first time since she came to the hospital, Erica managed to smile.

"Well, now, there's that beautiful smile I love to see; it lights up the room like sunshine," said Uncle Garwin cheerfully.

"I really miss being outside on a sunny day. Do you think I will ever see sunshine again?" asked Erica.

"We all hope you will get your sight back, and the doctors feel confident this is only a *temporary* situation. Nonetheless, you don't need to *see* the sun shining to know that it is there."

"What do you mean?"

"Think about all of the times you were resting on a blanket at the beach; you had your eyes closed, but you knew the sun was there because you could feel its warmth. . . . When I come back tomorrow, I will take you to the park next to the hospital. We'll have a picnic, and you can rest outside on a blanket and feel the warmth of the sun."

Realizing that she actually had something to look forward to in spite of her condition, Erica quickly sat up, grinning with anticipation.

A SOLAR ECLIPSE

"That will be SO MUCH FUN! I can pretend I am at the BEACH!" she shouted happily.

Uncle Garwin pulled a pair of peculiar sunglasses out of his pocket and put them on his niece. "Well, you'll need sunglasses if we are going to the beach!" he laughed.

"*Very* funny! How can the sun bother my eyes if I can't even see it?" asked Erica.

"That's the whole point! You *will* be able to feel the warmth of the sun, but you *won't* know exactly where it is. Therefore, you might accidentally look directly at the sun, and that can severely harm your eyes.... Do you remember what we did last year when a new moon came between Earth and the sun, causing a *solar eclipse?*"

"HUH? ... I remember I had to put my head inside of a cardboard box to watch the solar eclipse because ... uh, oh yeah, now I remember. I had to look at the solar eclipse through the box because looking right at the sun can hurt your eyes," said Erica.

"PRECISELY!" answered Uncle Garwin as he began to slowly pace back and forth across the room. "You had to look at an *image* of the solar eclipse on a white sheet of paper inside the box instead of looking *directly* at the solar eclipse."

Uncle Garwin's pacing speed changed from slow, weighty steps to quick, light strides while he began pointing his index finger back and forth—as if he were

9

teaching an important lesson in his classroom at the
university.

"The surface of the sun is called the *photosphere*.
Sometimes, a small part of the photosphere is still
visible during a solar eclipse, and looking at it can
harm your eyes, even if you are wearing sunglasses,"
he explained. "So, imagine how much *more* harmful
it would be to look right at the sun when there isn't a
solar eclipse!"

"I *am* glad you didn't bring a box to put over my
head when we go outside tomorrow, but *why* did you
bring sunglasses? I thought you said they can't protect
my eyes if I accidentally look at the sun!"

"That is true," answered Uncle Garwin. "Ordinary
sunglasses cannot completely protect your eyes if you
look directly at the sun, and you will need to make
sure you close your eyes if you tilt your head backwards when we go outside tomorrow. Nevertheless,
these are not *ordinary* sunglasses; they are
extraordinary sunglasses that were created especially
for you! Actually, they are an *old* pair of sunglasses
your mother gave to me. However, I made them more
effective by putting aluminum foil on the lenses."

"What will that do?" asked Erica.

"The foil will reflect the sunlight. You see,
reflected light is light that bounces off of something
like a mirror or aluminum foil.

"So the pieces of aluminum foil on the lenses are

A SOLAR ECLIPSE

like two mirrors; and they will protect my eyes by
reflecting the sun's rays," replied Erica in a scholarly
manner.

"That's an incredibly *reflective* thought!" laughed
Uncle Garwin.

"Thanks, I thought it 'mirrored' my true intelligence,"
joked Erica cheerfully as she began feeling the surface
of each lens with her index finger.

"How come some parts are really smooth and other
parts are crumply?" she asked.

Uncle Garwin grinned.

"I was wondering when you were going to notice
that! I put several reflective stickers on the aluminum
foil to prevent damage from sharp objects," he
boasted.

"You mean like finger nails? I'll try to be careful!"
promised Erica. "What kind of stickers did you put on
the aluminum foil?"

"All of your favorites. There is an astronaut, a
space shuttle, several stars, and two planets. . . . Can
you find them?" asked Uncle Garwin.

Erica rested her head back against the pillow and
began touching the smooth surface of each sticker very
gently with her fingers.

"There sure are a lot of stars! This is FUN! It's like
a blindfolded treasure hunt! The space shuttle feels
like it's on the right lens, and there is a big planet next
to it on the left. The astronaut is over here on the top

left lens . . . WOW! This planet next to the astronaut has BIG rings! Is it SATURN? And is the other planet JUPITER?" she asked.

"You guessed it! Saturn is on the left and Jupiter is on the right. It is quite interesting, though, with the exception of Jupiter and Saturn, most of the stickers blend in quite well with the aluminum foil when you look at them. So I think most people might not find all of the stickers unless they bothered to investigate by touching them the way you did!"

"HA! I should be a detective! Thanks, Uncle Garwin. These are radical! I can't wait to wear them outside tomorrow," said Erica, smiling.

"I'm glad you like them. I thought you might want to think of the Jupiter and Saturn stickers as your symbols of *hope* for your future, because before you know it, you will have your sight back and you'll be at the observatory experiencing a fantastic view of Jupiter and Saturn," assured Uncle Garwin.

"I hope so."

"Until then, remember something, Erica. Just like a solar eclipse, your lack of sight is only *temporary*. So think of this time in your life as a SOLAR ECLIPSE!" suggested Uncle Garwin.

"Oh, that makes sense. I'll just pretend this is a very *long* solar eclipse!"

"THAT'S the spirit! Now, I still have a couple of hours to stay and visit. Would you like to hear a story?"

A SOLAR ECLIPSE

"I SURE WOULD!"

There were so many things that Erica could not do anymore, but it was a sudden comfort for her to realize that Uncle Garwin's creative "science stories" could still be a part of her life.

"Which one would you like to hear?"

"I want to hear *The Cosmic Family*," replied Erica. "It's my favorite story because it's about the planets, and every time you tell it to me you add more awesome things about space to it."

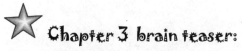 **Chapter 3 brain teaser:**

Why is the sun's gravity like a space map?

~ Chapter 3 ~

THE COSMIC FAMILY

WITH a big grin on her face, Erica contentedly leaned back against her pillow and tugged the covers up to her chin; she was ready to hear her uncle's story.

"FAR OUT IN THE VASTNESS OF THE UNIVERSE, 26,000 light years from the center of the Milky Way Galaxy, there is a unique SOLAR SYSTEM known as the *COSMIC FAMILY*," began Uncle Garwin.

THE COSMIC FAMILY

"This very special family has a brilliant, golden star, nine planets, and more than 100 moons," continued Uncle Garwin.

"The star is **Great-Grandmother Sun**. She is the *oldest* member of the family and exceedingly *wise*. This glorious sun knows many secrets of the universe and loves to tell stories she has heard from traveling comets.

"Great-Grandmother Sun is a spectacular, glowing star who radiates *heat* and *light* billions of miles into space. The heat from Great-Grandmother Sun gives the planets warmth, and her brilliant light gives the planets daytime. Furthermore, the light from Great-Grandmother Sun illuminates the planets in the darkness of space, so they appear to be sparkling stars in the night sky.

"With a massive radius of approximately 695,500 kilometers, Great-Grandmother Sun is about ten times larger than the biggest planet in the family, and 600 times larger than the smallest planet in the family.

"Great-Grandmother Sun also has the most powerful *gravity* in the Cosmic Family. Her strong gravity pulls all of the planets toward her in space, giving each planet its own invisible path around her called an *orbit*."

GREAT-
GRANDMOTHER

~ SUN ~

"For a very long time, people believed that Great-Grandmother Sun and the planets revolved around Earth, and most people didn't take kindly to theories that suggested otherwise. However, some astronomers throughout the centuries dared to believe in the *heliocentric theory*, which suggested that Earth and the planets actually revolve around Great-Grandmother Sun," said Uncle Garwin as he continued telling *The Cosmic Family* to Erica.

"As far back as the year 280 B.C., a Greek astronomer named *Aristarchus* stated his belief that Earth and the planets revolve around Great-Grandmother Sun. Unfortunately, his theory was not taken seriously. Then, around the year A.D.1514, a Polish astronomer named *Nicolaus Copernicus* wrote a small book for his friends. In the book he also stated the heliocentric theory, suggesting that Earth and the planets revolve around Great-Grandmother Sun. Nevertheless, most people did not believe Copernicus either.

"Finally, in A.D.1609, an Italian astronomer named *Galileo Galilei* introduced astronomers to his simple, low-powered telescope. As a result, once people were able to get a magnified view of space, they began to consider the possibility that Earth and the planets revolve around Great-Grandmother Sun. Now we all know that Earth and the planets continually *revolve* around Great-Grandmother Sun. So, the

Cosmic Family is called a solar system because *solar* means 'from the *sun*.'

"Each planet travels around Great-Grandmother Sun in its own *orbit*—over and over and over again like speeding cars on a race track. . . . Uh, except the planets move quite a bit faster than racecars, and they never have to stop for fuel or new tires. In fact, the planets never stop for anything at all!" explained Uncle Garwin.

"The amount of time it takes a planet to revolve around Great-Grandmother Sun is the length of a *year* on that planet. Earth takes about 365 days to revolve around her great-grandmother, so a year lasts about 365 days on Earth."

"EXCEPT FOR A LEAP YEAR!" interrupted Erica excitedly. "I know that because February 29th is my birthday. I only have a *real* birthday every four years when we have 366 days in a leap year, but Mom and Dad let me celebrate my birthday on February 28th when it isn't a leap year."

"You're certainly right about that," replied Uncle Garwin. "Every four years we need to have a leap year with 366 days because it actually takes Earth 365 days and about six hours to revolve around our Sun. . . . As a result, an extra six hours a year accumulated over a period of four years becomes a whole day, which is 24 hours. Therefore, every four years we add an extra day to the month of February and call it a leap year.

Adding the leap year allows us to keep our calendar synchronized with the time it takes Earth to revolve around our sun.

"Now, perhaps it may seem like a long time if you are waiting for a leap year to celebrate your *real* birthday, but it could be a longer wait between birthdays if you lived on a planet that is farther away from the sun. . . . Actually, if you lived on the planet that is usually farthest from the sun, you would never even have a chance to celebrate your *first* birthday—unless you lived for 248 'Earth-years.' "

"Whoa! I wouldn't like that!" replied Erica.

"Indeed, it definitely would seem unusual if we never had a chance to celebrate a birthday. . . .Well, now, let's continue with the story.

"Great-Grandmother Sun's gravity keeps the planets constantly revolving around her, which prevents them from getting lost in space and allows the planets and their powerful sun to stay together as a family," continued Uncle Garwin.

"Yet, the planets need to be extremely skilled at doing two things at once because revolving isn't the only thing the planets are doing out there in space. As a point of fact, the planets are all GIGANTIC spheres, and as each planet revolves in its orbit around Great-Grandmother Sun, it continually *rotates* on an invisible axis. . . . That means each planet spins around and around and around, kind of like an enormous spinning top. Ha! I must say, it reminds me of a candy

apple on a stick when you try to take a bite out of it!"
remarked Uncle Garwin, with a slight chuckle.

"Nonetheless, the amount of time it takes a planet
to rotate on its invisible axis is generally the length of
a *day* on that planet," he continued. "It takes Earth
about 24 hours to rotate on her invisible axis, so a day
on Earth is 24 hours.

"Now, while all of this is going on, the moons are
busy too! Like the planets, each moon rotates on an
invisible axis. Each moon also revolves in an orbit,
but there is a very important difference! Unlike the
planets, the moons in the Cosmic Family do not have
orbits that revolve around Great-Grandmother Sun . . .
the *moons* have orbits that *revolve* around the planets
they are closest to in the Cosmic Family. That is
because the gravity of each planet is strong enough to
keep its moon (or moons) from wandering away.
However, there is one moon who is so close to a
planet, she actually shares an orbit with that particular
planet.

"I must say, with the combination of Great-Grandmother Sun radiating heat and light—and the planets
and moons rotating and revolving, the Cosmic Family
experiences an abundance of constant activity. . . .
Everyone must be 'having a ball' out there in space!"
laughed Uncle Garwin.

⭐ **Chapter 4 brain teaser:** Erica has a
shepherd named Moon, and Mother Saturn has . . . ?

~ Chapter 4 ~

THE OUTER PLANETS

LISTENING to *The Cosmic Family* reminded Erica of how thrilling it would be to blast away from Earth and travel into space.

"It sounds totally awesome out there in space, and it's my biggest dream to go there someday," she said. "I want to travel all around our solar system and get close enough to see what everything out there really looks like! I would get to see Jupiter's moons, Saturn's rings and . . . I . . . I guess I wouldn't see *anything* because I CAN'T see anything! I don't know if I will ever be an astronaut or even get to go to the observatory!" she whimpered. "I really hate being blind!"

"I know this is hard for you, but I am sure everything is going to work out okay. Remember, Jupiter and Saturn are your symbols of *hope* for the future," replied Uncle Garwin, earnestly trying to console his niece.

Erica's uncle sat down on the hospital bed and gently held her hands. "You *will* get to see them, I promise," he said kindly. "Now, instead of thinking about yourself as someone who cannot see anything, try to focus on that incredible imagination you have. Imagine yourself in a gigantic spacecraft, soaring through the darkness of space. Then as I explain each planet, imagine it in your mind, and make it as *extraordinary* and *amazing* as you want it to be. . . . Can you give it a try?"

"Okay," sighed Erica.

"Then, on with our space journey!"

"**Uncle Pluto** is the smallest planet in the family. His largest moon is named *Charon*. Together Uncle Pluto and Charon are the planet and moon who share an orbit," stated Uncle Garwin.

"Uncle Pluto was discovered in 1930 by an astronomer named *Clyde Tombaugh*. By now, most people know Uncle Pluto as the ninth planet from Great-Grandmother Sun. Actually, MOST of the time he *is* farther away from Great-Grandmother Sun than any of the other planets in the family, so they call him 'far out'

Uncle Pluto. Because Uncle Pluto is so 'far out,' the HUBBLE SPACE TELESCOPE and the INFRARED ASTRONOMICAL SATELLITE (IRAS) have been very helpful to astronomers trying to learn more about him and Charon," continued Uncle Garwin.

"One unusual fact we know about Uncle Pluto is that he has an eccentric, elliptical orbit which takes him as far as 7,400,000,000 kilometers from Great-Grandmother Sun, or as close as 4,340,000,000 kilometers—a difference of about three billion kilometers! . . . Now, when Uncle Pluto is farther away from Great-Grandmother Sun, he gets covered with ice as his frigid temperatures drop as low as -230 degrees Celsius. Nevertheless, he loves to be that 'far out' because he enjoys a closer view of the *Kuiper Belt*, where he is determined to discover a new comet. He also likes to keep an eye on distant relatives farther out in space.

"Nonetheless, when Uncle Pluto's elliptical orbit brings him closer to Great-Grandmother Sun, he is quite thrilled also. Then he becomes the eighth planet from Great-Grandmother Sun, and he enjoys taking a 20-year 'solar vacation' as his icy surface begins to melt.

"The length of a day on Uncle Pluto is a whopping 154 hours because that's how long it takes him to rotate on his invisible axis . . . AND a year lasts 248 'Earth-years' because it takes him that long to make a complete orbit around Great-Grandmother Sun! . . ."

UNCLE

~ PLUTO ~

"Now then," said Uncle Garwin as he readily continued his story, "**Grandfather Neptune** is the eighth planet from Great-Grandmother Sun, except when Uncle Pluto comes closer for his 'solar vacation.' When that happens, which it recently did from January 1979, through February 1999, Grandfather Neptune becomes the ninth planet from Great-Grandmother Sun.

"Grandfather Neptune has a splendid bluish glow and very thin, mysterious rings. It takes him about 165 'Earth-years' to make one complete orbit around Great-Grandmother Sun and about 19 hours to rotate on his invisible axis. His radius is about 24,760 kilometers, which makes him the smallest of the four 'gas giants' in the family—but in truth, his radius is still 21 times *larger* than Uncle Pluto's radius!

"Grandfather Neptune was first observed in 1846 by a German astronomer named *Johann Gallee*, and we now know there are at least one dozen moons orbiting Grandfather Neptune. However, sometimes he forgets their names because his memory is fading a little. As a result of this, Grandfather Neptune gave his moons funny nicknames that help him remember who they are . . . like 'Tremendous' *Triton,* who is his largest moon and 'Nimble' *Naiad,* who is his closest moon. Naiad also orbits completely around Grand- father Neptune in the record-breaking Neptune 'moon orbit' time of seven hours and six minutes."

GRANDFATHER

~ NEPTUNE ~

"Moving closer to Great-Grandmother Sun, we find **Grandmother Uranus**," smiled Uncle Garwin, "and I must say, she is quite beautiful! She is a glowing, bluish-green planet who is adorned with rings made of ice and dust. In 1781, a British astronomer named *William Herschel* discovered Grandmother Uranus; although when he first found her, Hershel thought he had discovered a comet.

"Grandmother Uranus is the seventh planet from Great-Grandmother Sun, and it takes her about 84 'Earth-years' to make a complete orbit. Like Grandfather Neptune, she is also a 'gas giant.' However, she has a radius of about 25,560 kilometers, which makes her even larger than Grandfather Neptune!

"Unfortunately, she had a serious accident a long time ago, which left her tipped on her side. Nonetheless, Grandmother Uranus still manages to rotate on her invisible axis in about 18 hours, even though she does it backwards!

"Grandmother Uranus has at least 27 moons. She is particularly fond of her largest moon, *Titania*, and her brightest moon, *Ariel*. That's because her eyesight is not what it used to be, so Titania and Ariel are the easiest moons for her to see out in space. Nevertheless, both grandparents are very proud of all their rings and moons, and you can often find the two of them gazing into space admiring their beauty."

GRANDMOTHER

~ URANUS ~

Erica began to think about her own grandparents sitting on the front porch gazing at stars in the evening sky and admiring their beauty. This vivid memory of her grandparents was pleasant at first, but then she remembered that her grandparents' porch was the last familiar place she saw before they took her to the hospital.

Trying to ignore the unpleasant memory that was creeping into her mind, Erica made an admirable effort to envision the planets with her imagination, as her uncle had suggested.

. . . I just passed Neptune. . . . Now I am gliding by Uranus. She is a beautiful, GIANT gas planet. . . . Bluish-green is my favorite color, like the ocean. Uranus's rings look like diamond necklaces . . . thought Erica, trying her best to enjoy the story and ignore her unpleasant memories.

"The orbits of **Father Jupiter** and **Mother Saturn** are between the orbits of the grandparents and the children. Father Jupiter and Mother Saturn are also 'gas giants' with rings," continued Uncle Garwin.

However, despite Erica's effort, she was finding it difficult to enjoy the story and ignore her gloomy thoughts. . . . THEN, as she focused on those gloomy thoughts, Erica began to experience angry feelings stirring inside her.

. . . JUPITER! . . . SATURN! . . . My favorite planets! I could have seen them at the OBSERVATORY! Mark SHOULD NOT have told the SECRET about my ACCIDENT! . . . she thought angrily. *I AM REALLY MAD! . . . IT WAS A SECRET!*

Uncle Garwin noticed that Erica's arms were firmly clasped around her waist, and her lips were tightly pressed together . . . all scrunched up like she just bit into a fresh, sour lemon. He assumed she was pre-occupied with sad thoughts about Moon . . . the observatory . . . her blindness. However, he decided it was best to continue the story, hoping it would distract Erica from her troubling thoughts.

"The sixth planet from Great-Grandmother Sun is **Mother Saturn**, one of your favorite planets!" continued Uncle Garwin enthusiastically. "In the early sixteenth century, *Galileo Galilei* discovered rings around Mother Saturn while looking through his telescope. These icy rings colorfully decorate her like whirling rainbows in space, and they are considered to be the most beautiful rings in the family. We now know that Mother Saturn's rings are about a mile thick and quite wide. In fact, her rings are so wide, if Mother Saturn and her rings happened to be out there in space between Earth and Earth's moon, one end of her rings would reach Earth . . . and the other end would reach Earth's moon!

"Mother Saturn is also fortunate enough to have over 30 moons swiftly twirling around her. Her largest moon, named *Titan,* happens to be bigger than Uncle Pluto is! She also has two very special moons called *Shepherd* moons because they help keep the outermost part of Mother Saturn's rings together as she spins through space.

"It takes her about 30 'Earth-years' to make a complete orbit around Great-Grandmother Sun, but it only takes her 10.2 hours to rotate on her invisible axis. She is larger than either of the grandparents, and her radius is approximately 60,270 kilometers, which qualifies her as a *humongous* 'gas giant.' "

MOTHER

~ SATURN ~

VOICES IN THE DARK

"The last of the outer planets is **Father Jupiter**, your other favorite planet!" remarked Uncle Garwin cheerfully. "Known for his *stormy* 'red eye,' Father Jupiter is the fifth planet from Great-Grandmother Sun. It takes him about 11 'Earth-years' to make a complete orbit around her and about 9.8 hours to rotate on his invisible axis. Although his rings are very thin, he is the largest 'gas giant' which also makes him the largest planet in the family. In fact, if he were hollow, all of the other planets would fit inside of him! His radius is about 71,490 kilometers, so he is around one tenth the size of Great-Grandmother Sun!

"FATHER JUPITER has more than 60 moons! Surrounding him like bees circling a hive, these spectacular moons enhance the magnificence of this planet and create a remarkable spectacle in space. His largest moons are *Io, Europa, Ganymede* and *Callisto*. All theses moons were discovered by the famous astronomer, *Galileo Galilei*. *Io* has spouting volcanoes that are exceptionally active, icy *Europa* has the brightest and smoothest surface, *Ganymede* is the largest moon, and *Callisto* has the most craters.

"Nonetheless, some of Jupiter's smaller moons are amazing too. *Amalthea, Metis, Thebe* and *Adrastea* are small oddly shaped moons who are helping Jupiter maintain his rings, which is a tough job for small moons! Amalthea also has the most dynamic crimson color of any moon in the family."

34

FATHER

~ JUPITER ~

"Unlike the grandparents, however, when Father Jupiter and Mother Saturn gaze into space, it's not because they are admiring rings and moons. They gaze into space because they are guarding their children from *asteroids*, which are huge rocks that fly around in space," continued Uncle Garwin.

As she listened to her uncle talking about *moons* and *rocks*, Erica's stirring anger seized control of her thoughts, and her mind finally wandered *completely* away from Uncle Garwin's story. . . .

. . . *That STUPID ROCK! . . . I just hope mom and dad don't blame MOON for this!* thought Erica, feeling as if she was going to burst apart from anger. . . .

. . . *Do they really think it IS MOON'S fault? . . . Did they find ANOTHER home for MOON?* she suddenly wondered as her anger rapidly changed to fear.

. . . I am AFRAID mom and dad WON'T tell me the TRUTH about it while I'm in the HOSPITAL! I can't know for sure if I'm not at home . . . home . . . hey . . . Matthew . . . Matthew's at home.

Then, for a brief moment, Erica's fear faded because she had a plan.

. . . I know what to do! I can ask Matthew! I know he'll tell me the truth because he's a BIG BLABBERMOUTH! . . . There, that takes care of THAT problem, she thought hopefully. *. . . NOW I can listen to Uncle Garwin's story.*

Erica made a genuine effort to relax and listen to her favorite story, but as she heard the words *Jupiter* and *Saturn,* she felt tears swelling in her eyes.

. . . I know Uncle Garwin told me that JUPITER and SATURN should be my symbols of HOPE, but listening to the story keeps reminding me of my accident, she realized sorrowfully.

. . . I need to think of a way to get Uncle Garwin to stop telling the story without letting him know that I'm really upset about my accident. . . . Oh, I know what to say!

"Uncle Garwin, I'm *hungry!*" mumbled Erica.

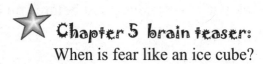

Chapter 5 brain teaser:
When is fear like an ice cube?

~ Chapter 5 ~

POSITIVELY

WITHOUT a doubt, Erica *was* hungry. On top everything else that had been making her miserable, she did not like the food at the hospital and had barely eaten anything since she got there.

"The food here is really YUCKY! It's runny and mushy, and they never have pizza," complained Erica.

"I'm feeling quite hungry myself, and pizza would just hit the spot! Lie back and rest for a little while, and I'll be back with a delicious pizza before you even have a chance to miss me."

Unfortunately, Erica felt lonely as soon as her uncle left, and it seemed like it was taking *forever* for him to come back. Shutting her eyes tightly in an attempt to squish the persistent tears, Erica waited alone in the dark for her uncle to return.

"I have a PIZZA delivery for a brave scientist," said Uncle Garwin cheerfully.

"I am really glad you're back," sobbed Erica. "I felt so lonely when you weren't here, and you *always* seem to say the right thing to make me feel better."

"I wish I could stay with you until you go home, but we both know that isn't possible. This is a time in your life when it is very important for you to believe that you are *brave* enough to endure whatever happens while you are in the hospital. . . . Now, remember, we talked about how this time in your life could be like a *solar eclipse*," mentioned Uncle Garwin kindly.

"Yes, I KNOW! It's only TEMPORARY!" snapped Erica irritably. "But I don't like the darkness when you're not here!"

"Well, try to think of it from another point of view. When there is a solar eclipse, it gets dark because the moon passes in front of the sun, but the sun is still there, *right?"*

"RIGHT, but I *don't* get what you're talking about!" retorted Erica. She slouched down under the covers, barely listening to her uncle as discontented thoughts rambled through her mind.

. . . *This solar eclipse stuff is getting boring. I wish he would just stop talking about it!* she thought.

Uncle Garwin began to quickly pace back and forth, pointing his "professor finger" toward a very reluctant student.

"Even though it gets darker on Earth during a solar eclipse," he said, "the sun is still behind the moon shining in space, and it can be that way for you too. Even though there is darkness in your life because of your blindness, you can still believe that the sun is shining in your *mind* and try to keep a *positive attitude.*"

Erica had to restrain herself from rudely expressing disinterest in her uncle's solar eclipse lesson.

. . . *This seems pointless! What am I supposed to believe about the sun?* she wondered sarcastically.

Then, before she could catch herself, Erica grumbled out loudly.

"WHAT DO YOU MEAN?" she yelled.

. . . *Whoops! Why did I ask him that?* she thought. *Now he's going to keep talking about an eclipse, my blindness, and whatever else he comes up with!*

Still pacing and pointing, Uncle Garwin continued his "mini-lecture."

"Well, if you think about everything that you *don't* like, you are creating *negative* thoughts. However, if you try to think about what you *do* like, then you are creating *positive* thoughts. Think of the positive thoughts as the SUN shining behind the darkness," he told her.

. . . Okay! . . . That's enough of this POSITIVE, SUNSHINE STUFF! It all sounds like mumbo jumbo to me, thought Erica gruffly.

Reluctant to believe that thinking about sunshine could change her circumstances, Erica sat up and scowled at her uncle.

"What DIFFERENCE does it make? I can't THINK my way out of being a BLIND person stuck in the HOSPITAL!" complained Erica cantankerously, and then she swiftly flung her head back against the pillow.

Uncle Garwin sat next to Erica and held onto her hands again. He knew she was not the least bit interested in the *positive* and *negative* idea, but he attempted to reason with her anyway.

"You're right, you cannot think your way out of the hospital, but you can try to make the *best* of it while you are here—and having a positive attitude can help you to feel brave."

The word *brave* stuck in Erica's mind.

. . . It can help me to feel BRAVE? . . . Hmm,
she mused. *I guess he really is trying to help me.*
Maybe I should listen to what he's saying.

"How can it do *that*?" asked Erica.

"Your *feelings* come from your *thoughts*,"
explained Uncle Garwin. "It's kind of like a road map
in your mind. If you want to *feel* joyful, take the
'thought road' that will get you to '**JOY**TOWN' rather
than . . . uh . . . allowing your thoughts to take you to
'**FEAR**VILLE' or '**SAD**' CITY," he chortled.

"Seriously though, if you think *negative* thoughts,
then you will have *negative* feelings. As a result, if
you *think* you are afraid, then you will *feel* afraid.
On the other hand . . . if you think *positive* thoughts,
then you will have *positive* feelings. Therefore, if
you *tell* yourself you are brave, you will begin to
feel brave. Then, when you feel brave, the things you
were afraid of start to melt away like ice cubes in the
sun."

"It's like the 'Wicked Witch of the West' in *The
Wizard of Oz*," remarked Erica. "Dorothy was totally
afraid of that horrible witch. But Dorothy was brave,
so she did what she had to do to get back home—and she
really *did* make the witch melt away."

"That is a brilliant *analogy*!" replied Uncle Garwin.

Erica grinned confidently.

"I thought about something else too. Do you think

what's happening to me is kind of like a *lunar eclipse*?" she asked.

"You mean when the full moon passes through Earth's shadow, and it gets really dark outside because we cannot see the moon?"

"Uh . . . yep, that's what I mean."

"Why does your situation remind you of a lunar eclipse?" asked Uncle Garwin curiously.

"Because during a lunar eclipse it is really dark and you cannot see the full moon, but it is still there in space," replied Erica.

"That's certainly true," agreed Uncle Garwin.

"So right now it's really dark for *ME* too because I'm blind," continued Erica, "and I also have to be without *MOON*, but he is still there at home—well, at least I *hope* he is!"

"Thinking of your situation as a lunar eclipse certainly is another *fantastic* analogy! If you keep coming up with great analogies like that one, I'll have to take you to the university to teach a class about it!" declared Uncle Garwin.

"I'll do ANYTHING to get out of the hospital!" replied Erica lightheartedly. "And I guess I do understand what you were trying to explain to me about having positive thoughts. . . . If I *tell* myself I am *afraid* of the darkness, it means I am having *negative* thoughts, and I will *feel* afraid. But if I tell myself I am brave, it means I am having *positive* thoughts, and it will help me not to *feel* afraid of the darkness."

Relieved that his niece finally understood the "positive attitude" lesson, Uncle Garwin smiled contentedly, and he vigorously began shaking Erica's hand.

"INGENIOUS PERCEPTION! I can see that you are already trying to apply my advice to your situation," he said.

"But do you really think having a positive attitude will work for me while I'm in the hospital?"

"*POSITIVELY!* Keep telling yourself you are brave—and try to think about things you *like* when you get scared. Then your mind will be so busy with positive thoughts, it won't have any room for the negative stuff. Trust in this and soon you will find yourself feeling *very* brave. And believe it or not, once you stop feeling so afraid, you'll be able to appreciate your *other* senses more than ever," said Uncle Garwin.

"Well my SENSES tell me that I SMELL pizza," laughed Erica, "and I am totally FAMISHED!"

The smell of pizza seemed to permeate every atom of her nostrils, and she could not remember a time when pizza smelled quite as appetizing as it did at that moment.

. . . Does being blind have anything to do with how totally awesome this pizza smells—or is it just

because I'm sooooooo hungry? wondered Erica, and then she took her first scrumptious bite. . . . *Yummmmm, this is totally delicious!*

⭐ **Chapter 6 brain teaser:**
Where can a day last longer than a year?

~ Chapter 6 ~

THE SOLAR
CHILDREN

WITH her stomach full and her mind at ease, Erica was anxious to hear the rest of *The Cosmic Family*.

"We might as well summarize the first part of the story together before I finish," suggested Uncle Garwin.

. . . He's right, thought Erica. *It isn't going to be exciting if I only hear the last part now. It would be like watching the end of a movie and missing some of the best parts. . . . What an awesome uncle! I guess he still remembers what it's like to be a kid. I am so lucky there's an adult around who THINKS like a kid and TALKS to me like I'm grown up enough to think for myself. He even believes that I can think my way into being brave . . .*

"Erica?"

"Huh? . . . Oh, sorry, I was daydreaming. It's a GREAT idea! Let's summarize, it wouldn't be very much fun to just hear the last part of my favorite story."

"You know, Erica, this is my favorite story too," replied Uncle Garwin. "Nine planets living together as a family and orbiting their Great-Grandmother Sun is truly something spectacular, and it's exciting to imagine that our planet, Earth, is part of a large family that lives out in space."

"And Earth has a curious 'far out' uncle, just like I do!" laughed Erica.

"Then there's Grandfather Neptune and Grandmother Uranus who love to admire their rings and moons," continued Uncle Garwin.

"Next there's Mother Saturn and Father Jupiter. Mother Saturn has beautifully colored rings, and

Father Jupiter has a *stormy* 'red eye'—plus more moons than any of the other planets," added Erica.

"That's correct. Father Jupiter and Mother Saturn are also the largest planets, and they have a significant job to do."

"I know . . . they guard the children from asteroids. That's where you stopped telling the story. I remember hearing about rocks because it reminded me of, uh . . . oh, never mind," sighed Erica, trying not to mention her accident again.

"Hey! Where are my sunglasses?" she asked, with a glowing smile.

"They are right here. Do you want them?"

"I want to wear them as a reminder that Jupiter and Saturn are symbols of hope for my future . . . and to remind myself to keep the SUN shining in my mind."

"Bright idea indeed," laughed Uncle Garwin as he handed the shiny sunglasses to his niece.

Erica gently placed the sunglasses on the bottom of her chin, slid both sides up to her ears, and carefully positioned the glasses across her nose. Then she leaned back onto her pillow and grinned.

"READY!" she yelled.

"LOOK OUT FOR FLYING ROCKS!" her uncle yelled back. . . .

"*Asteroids* are huge rocks that fly around in space," stated Uncle Garwin, continuing the story from where he had stopped for the "pizza break." "The radius of an asteroid can range from less than one kilometer to 470 kilometers, which is the radius of *Ceres*, the largest asteroid. In fact, Ceres and three of the other larger asteroids have a spherical shape and are quite 'moon-like.'

"Millions of asteroids orbit Great-Grandmother Sun in the ASTEROID BELT, located between Father Jupiter and the children. However, sometimes an asteroid from the Asteroid Belt may get knocked out of its orbit and head toward the children, so Father Jupiter tries to protect the children from speeding asteroids by keeping a close watch on the Asteroid Belt with his *stormy* 'red eye.' And Mother Saturn also keeps watch for asteroids that may be dangerously wandering aimlessly through space. That's because a very large, unknown asteroid once caused a terrible accident when it collided with Grandmother Uranus and tipped her onto her side.

"Now, speaking of the children, *Mars, Earth, Venus* and *Mercury* have orbits between the Asteroid Belt and Great-Grandmother Sun. They are closer to their great-grandmother than any of the other planets, so the adults in the family call them the 'solar children.' However, scientists classify them as *terrestrial* planets because they are small with a solid surface."

"**Mars** is known as the RED PLANET," stated Uncle Garwin. "His orbit is right next to the asteroid belt. And as the responsible, older brother, Mars helps his parents protect the other children from asteroids. So far, he has managed to capture two asteroids and keep them as his own moons. Mars has given his moons the names *Phobos* and *Deimos*.

"Mars's radius is 3,397 kilometers, which makes him a rather small planet, but he has the largest volcano in the entire family. It takes him about 687 days to revolve around his great-grandmother, which is nearly the length of two 'Earth-years.' He can rotate on his invisible axis in 24.6 hours; hence, a day on Mars lasts a little bit longer than a day on Earth.

"Scientists are very interested in sending different types of spacecrafts to explore Mars because they want to find clues about water and past or present types of life forms that might be there. In 1976, the first land exploration began when the *Viking* I and the *Viking* II successfully landed on Mars to search for life. Since then, the *Pathfinder* successfully landed on Mars in 1997, and in 2004, the *Opportunity* and the *Spirit* also landed on Mars. In the future, scientists hope to send the *Mars Science Laboratory* to learn more about the environment on Mars. Someday there may even be people *living* on Mars!"

~ MARS ~

"Next we come to our home planet, **Earth**," smiled Uncle Garwin. "Earth truly is a special planet. She has enough WATER, LAND, and AIR for millions of different 'types' of LIVING SPECIES to exist on her—and I must say, she is extremely fortunate to have such a beautiful environment. However, Earth's special environment needs constant care, which requires a lot of perseverance. Earth also needs to be quite creative, compassionate, and courageous because she has taken on the challenge of sharing her environment with billions of *Homo sapiens*!

"Her orbit is between Mars and Venus, so she is the third planet from Great-Grandmother Sun. In fact, Earth's orbit is approximately 150,000,000 kilometers away from her great-grandmother, and scientists refer to this distance as an *astronomical unit.*

"Earth looks like a magnificent, blue star sapphire as she whirls around her great-grandmother in space. Her radius is 6,378.14 kilometers, which makes her the largest of the children. It takes Earth approximately 365.25 days to revolve around Great-Grandmother Sun and about 24 hours to rotate on her invisible axis.

"Earth enjoys the privilege of having her very own moon named *Luna,* who likes to help Earth. Luna uses her gravity to help create tides in Earth's oceans, and she provides beautifully glowing light in Earth's dark night sky."

~ EARTH ~

"**Venus** is the younger of the two sisters and has an orbit between Earth and Mercury; therefore, she is the second planet from Great-Grandmother Sun," continued Uncle Garwin. "Even though Venus isn't the closest planet to Great-Grandmother Sun, she is the *hottest* planet. That's because her environment is filled with carbon dioxide, which holds onto heat.

"Covered with radiant yellow and orange swirls, Venus sparkles in space like a glistening topaz gem. Her radius is 6,051.8 kilometers, so she is just a little bit smaller than her older sister, Earth. Venus happens to be very fond of her older sister. She would do anything to help Earth and wants to be more like her, too. Venus especially wants to have her very own moon, just like Earth does—and she is quite tenacious about trying to catch one someday.

"In fact, Venus is so stubborn about capturing a passing asteroid and making it her own moon, she takes 243 days to *rotate* on her invisible axis . . . which means a day on Venus lasts 243 'Earth-days.' Furthermore, Venus rotates in a *clockwise* direction, which is opposite of the direction she travels when she *revolves* around Great-Grandmother Sun. You see, Venus wants to be certain that she looks thoroughly in every direction so she won't miss her chance to snag an asteroid. What's more, since it only takes Venus 225 'Earth-days' to revolve around her great-grandmother, a day on Venus is longer than a year on Venus."

~ *VENUS* ~

"Then last, but not least, there is the zealous, little brother, **Mercury**, whose orbit is right next to Great-Grandmother Sun. His radius is 2,439.7 kilometers, which makes him the smallest child. Like Uncle Pluto, he has a highly elliptical orbit that brings him as close as 47,000,000 kilometers and as far away as 70,000,000 kilometers from his great-grandmother," explained Uncle Garwin.

"It takes Mercury 58.7 'Earth-days' to rotate on his invisible axis. Nevertheless, every 88 days he completes a speedy orbit around Great-Grandmother Sun. Afterwards, he gets outrageously excited—constantly pestering his brother and sisters about how much longer it takes them to revolve around Great-Grandmother Sun.

"Mercury is a small planet who is covered with craters. He looks a lot like Earth's moon, and he is only about one and a half times larger than Luna. Mercury doesn't have a moon of his own, but just like Venus, he really wants a moon someday too. However, sometimes when Venus gets tired of listening to Mercury brag about how fast he can zoom around Great-Grandmother Sun, Venus reminds Mercury that she is bigger than him—and if he doesn't stop pestering her, she'll turn *him* into *her* moon."

~ MERCURY ~

"Even though Mercury is the closest planet to Great-Grandmother Sun," continued Uncle Garwin, "all the solar children cherish being as close as they are to their brilliantly glowing great-grandmother. . . . And, on very special evenings, the children feel especially warm and cozy as Great-Grandmother Sun tells the whole family her enchanting 'comet tales' of cosmic adventures in distant spirals of the galaxy.

"No one knows *exactly* how long the Cosmic Family has been in space, but for as long as anyone can remember, the planets and Great-Grandmother Sun have been a very happy family. . . THE END!"

⭐ **Chapter 7 brain teaser:**
What kind of paper feels like a candle?

~ Chapter 7 ~

THE SOS RECEIVER

"*UNCLE* Garwin, were you thinking about *our* family when you made up the story about the *Cosmic Family?*" asked Erica.

"Indeed, I was. I thought of it when I was sitting under the old tree in the forest behind your grand-parents' house. Actually, I was sitting there thinking about our solar system, and I guess I dozed off for a few minutes because I had an extremely vivid dream that the planets had feelings and personalities, just like our family," answered Uncle Garwin.

"I sit under that tree and think about our solar system, too. I sat there with Moon just before my accident . . . I was thinking about how much I wanted to visit the observatory," replied Erica, "and I was *totally* disappointed that I didn't get to go there with you that night. Besides, I didn't lose my sight until the next day. I just wish you hadn't found out that I hit my head until the next day either, so I could have gone with you."

"Well, as it turned out, none of us went to the observatory. There was a gas leak on the ground floor, which caused an explosion and a fire. Fortunately, no one was in the observatory when it happened," explained Uncle Garwin.

Astonished by the news, Erica quickly sat up and leaned forward.

"Did the fire happen when we were supposed to be there?" she asked curiously.

"Yes, it did. In fact, about an hour after we were due to arrive at the observatory, Professor Gazer, the astronomer in charge that night, left the observatory and went to the main office to find out if we were still coming. . . . The explosion happened while she was gone."

"YIKES! Professor Gazer was lucky!"

"Yes, we all were. You see, by bringing you here as soon as we did, the doctors were able to treat your injury and keep you from going blind permanently. If we had waited until the next day, your condition could have been more serious than it is. Furthermore, no one was injured by the explosion because no one was in the observatory," stated Uncle Garwin.

"Not even Professor Gazer, who was checking to find out why we didn't show up," added Erica.

"That is correct. I know we cannot always understand the reason things happen the way they do, nevertheless, that *does not* mean we should lose *hope*. Things always seem to have a way of working out in the end. I realize you have suffered from a very unfortunate accident—and believe me, we *all* wish it never happened."

Uncle Garwin sat down next to his niece and patted the blanket area covering her toes.

"However, to look at the situation from a *positive* point of view," he said, "it seems as if your accident helped prevent many people from being injured by a more serious accident. And, who knows what other good things may come from it?"

"I feel *important!*"

"ERICA TERRANO, you are important—and don't you *ever* forget it!"

Erica reached out to her uncle and gave him a big, warm hug.

"Thank you, Uncle Garwin . . . thanks for EVERY-THING!" she said gratefully.

"You are quite welcome, but I'm not ready to go just yet. I would not want to leave without giving you the surprise I've been working on."

Erica immediately began to bombard her uncle with questions.

"A SURPRISE? Do you have it with you? Can I have it *now*? What is it?" she asked eagerly.

"Indeed I do . . . yes you can . . . and here it is," said Uncle Garwin, placing a strange, glossy box on his niece's lap.

Erica was surprised when she felt the box. "Is this real wrapping paper? It feels weird!"

. . . *Of course it isn't*, she thought. *Uncle Garwin always wraps presents with some kind of used paper—he calls it RECYCLING. . . . Most of the time he uses the comic section of the newspaper, and once he used the back of a paper bag and then taped pictures of Mars on the top. . . . But this doesn't feel*

THE SOS RECEIVER

like a paper bag or news paper, it feels like a square candle.

Uncle Garwin chuckled lightheartedly.

"Ah . . . technically speaking, it *is* wrapping paper because it is a type of *paper,* and it is *wrapped* around the box," he said. "However, you are right; it is also unusual, and I must say, I never used it before. I . . . uh, I guess that could be due to the fact that I never gave a gift to someone who was not going to *look* at the way it was wrapped."

"I can't believe I'm more interested in what my gift is *wrapped* in than what the gift *is*!" said Erica. "You were right; I am paying more attention to my other senses. If I wasn't blind, I would have opened this gift by now to find out what's inside the box!"

Erica kept sliding her fingers back and forth across the smooth surface.

"It feels like a big candle," she said. ". . . Hey, wait a minute, I know what this is! It's WAX PAPER isn't it!?! You can see through wax paper, but I *can't* see, so it doesn't matter!"

"*Phenomenal* conclusion, Erica!"

"Did you know I would try to figure out what my present was wrapped in before I opened it?"

"Well, I certainly know how curious you are, so I had a hunch you would have some fun with it," admitted Uncle Garwin.

"Do you really save wax paper and use it again?"

"If it can be *reused*, I use it again!" replied Uncle Garwin. "Now go ahead and open the box—see if you can guess what's inside of it."

Erica quickly ripped the wax paper off the box.

"Oops! . . . You weren't going to recycle this, were you?" She burst into laughter. "I never had so much fun just *opening* a present!"

Finally pulling the gift out of the box, Erica gently touched every part of it. Then she said, "It feels like a CD player . . . and it has headphones! THANK YOU, I love it!"

"You are quite close," said Uncle Garwin. "It used to be a CD player, but I altered the technology on the inside and now it is something that is quite a bit more unusual than a CD player. I have actually been working on it for several years, but after your accident, I wanted to get it finished for you. That is the reason it took me so long to come visit you. I knew you were disappointed that you couldn't go to the observatory, so I thought this gift might help you feel a little bit better about it."

"What does it do?" inquired Erica.

"My invention is actually a space receiver. It detects sounds in space and directs them through this machine. I call it the *SOS RECEIVER*, which is short for *'Sounds Of Space' RECEIVER*," explained Uncle Garwin.

"This is RADICAL! Does it really work?"

"Actually, I haven't had a chance to try it out yet—but according to my calculations, it should do what it is programmed to do."

"I can't wait to try it! How does it work?"

"There are only two regulating buttons that you will need to use, and you can find them easily with your fingers," said Uncle Garwin. "There is a blank CD in the machine, which will allow you to record sounds, but right now I have it set so you can listen through the headphones."

Uncle Garwin placed Erica's index finger on the first button. "This will turn it on, and the button on the right will turn it off," he said.

"Let me try it! . . . PLEASE! Can I try it?" begged Erica.

However, just as Uncle Garwin was helping Erica use the SOS RECEIVER for the very first time, Matthew came running through the door, followed close behind by Erica's parents and Valen.

 Chapter 8 brain teaser:
When can something be different and the same?

~ Chapter 8 ~

NEW MOON

ERICA'S parents immediately began fussing over her with warm greetings, hugs, and a soft, new pillow covered with a freshly washed pillowcase—which they thoroughly fluffed and comfortably placed behind her head. Matthew, on the other hand, made a direct beeline for the SOS Receiver.

Uncle Garwin rushed over to him instantly.

"Hi, Erica, what do you have there?" he asked quietly.

"I'M NOT ERICA!" snapped Matthew.

Uncle Garwin stooped down next to Matthew and

whispered into his ear. "Oh, I thought you were Erica, because that is her gift you are holding. Did you ask her if you could play with it?"

"N o o o . . ." grumbled Matthew while scowling at his uncle and mischievously holding the SOS Receiver behind his back.

"Then let's leave her gift alone for now, okay buddy?" Uncle Garwin said patiently, and then he held out his hand in front of Matthew.

"O-KAY," groaned Matthew. He reluctantly handed the receiver to his uncle, flopped onto the floor and sat there pouting for a full two seconds. After which he picked up a small, but colorful paper bag off the floor and hopped up onto Erica's bed.

"I have a gift for Erica, too!" he boasted.

Matthew took a quick look at Erica and roared with laughter.

"Hey, how come you're wearing those FUNNY glasses?" he yelled.

"They happen to be . . . uh, very special *astronaut* glasses," remarked Erica, with quite an annoyed tone in her voice.

"OH, COOL! Can *I* wear them?"

Erica leaned forward and shook her head.

"No, they wouldn't fit you," she answered dryly.

"Hey, that's NOT FAIR! I want to wear astronaut glasses too! *Mom*, can I get *astronaut* glasses? . . . CAN I? . . . PLEASE!" begged Matthew.

"We'll see," answered Mrs.Terrano. "Why don't you give Erica the gift you have for her?"

"Here, this is for you," said Matthew, plopping the bag on Erica's lap. "It's a big bag with lots of candy in it. Mom says you can feel the pieces to guess what kind they are and smell them to guess what flavor they are before you eat them. Can I have some?"

"Sure, just don't eat all of it. . . . Sooo . . . Matthew, how is MOON? Did you see him before you came here?" asked Erica as casually as she could, even though she couldn't wait to hear his answer.

"Yep, he was in your room," answered Matthew, and then he popped a whole piece of candy in his mouth.

Erica was *elated!* She flopped her head back onto her new, soft pillow and grinned from ear to ear, *almost* as blissfully as if *Moon* was right in the room with her.

. . . *It must be true,* she thought. *Matthew always blabs whenever he knows about something. . . . I am so happy! . . . Moon was in my room! My parents didn't get rid of him!*

"Moon is doing pretty good," added Valen. "I've been petting him a lot and playing with him in the yard, but I think he misses you because he still sleeps in your room every night."

Valen sat down next to Erica and carefully placed a black and tan stuffed animal on her lap.

"Here . . . I brought this for you. It's a German shepherd," she said, with a proud smile.

Erica wrapped her arms around the fluffy, new present and rubbed her face across the soft fur.

"Thanks so much. I really like it!"

"What are you going to name it?" asked Valen excitedly.

"Well, he *is* a German shepherd, like Moon. And he's *new* . . . so I guess I will name him 'NEW' *Moon*. Oh, plus I can't *see* him, and you can't *see* a *new moon* either," added Erica.

"*New Moon* . . . I like that!" Valen leaned over, looked into the stuffed animal's plastic, amber eyes, and started to pet him on the head.

"Hi, New Moon. . . . Do you like your new name?" she asked softly.

"I like *New Moon,* too! WAY TO GO, Erica! That is also ANOTHER great *analogy*," said Uncle Garwin, in a very complimentary way.

"What's algae?" asked Matthew.

"It's an *A-NAL-O-GY!*" snapped Valen. "If you'd pay attention to what we're saying instead of that bag of candy. . ."

Matthew shuffled backwards to the big chair on the other side of the room as he held the bag of candy behind his back.

"Hey, there, **VALERIE NADINE**, I bet *YOU* don't even know what it means!" he yelled, with a devious grin.

"Don't call me that! And, I do too *know* what it means! I learned it at school! It means . . . it means they are . . . uh . . . *different* and the *same!*" shouted Valen tenaciously.

Matthew plopped down onto the big chair and burst into laughter.

"HA! . . . HA! . . . HA! . . . I *knew* you didn't know what it means! . . . How can something be the *same* if it's *different?*" he retorted.

"Actually, Valen is right," said Uncle Garwin. "An *analogy* refers to things that can be very different from each other but still have at least one thing that is the same. . . . An example would be if I said Matthew is like a *rocket!* Now I know you do not *look* like a rocket, or *smell* like a rocket. Actually, a rocket is a form of technology and you are a person . . ."

Uncle Garwin started laughing loudly.

"However, both *you* and a *rocket* make a lot of NOISE!" he said jokingly. "AND, a rocket can *zoom* into space, and you like to *zoom* through the house . . . or the yard . . . or wherever you go for that matter!" he chuckled.

"YEA! I'M A ROCKET!" shouted Matthew.

"Where's Mark?" asked Erica as she began to wonder why her older brother hadn't come to visit her.

"He is at Nana and Grandpa's house working on a science report that is due tomorrow. I am sure he will come to see you after he is finished," answered Mrs.Terrano.

Erica wondered . . . *Maybe Mark thinks I am still mad at him, or maybe Mark is mad at me. . . . Maybe that is the real reason he's not here!*

"Why hasn't he come to visit me yet?" questioned Erica suspiciously.

"He *did* come with us yesterday, but you were sleeping. The nurse said that we should not wake you, so Nana and Grandpa took Valen, Mark, and Matthew to their house, and we stayed here until you woke up," explained Mrs. Terrano.

"Oh," replied Erica very quietly, still uncertain about the whole situation. She wanted to know if everything was okay between her and Mark. After all, the last thing Erica said to him was . . . "You are a BIG TATTLETALE!"

Valen moved closer to Erica and started to tickle her feet.

"This is from Mark. He said to tell you that he misses you, and he hopes you will be home from the hospital soon," she said between giggles.

"Hey, stop that!" laughed Erica. "What is his report about anyway? Is it about something in space?"

"No, it's about *pollution*, a problem right here on our own planet," answered Mr. Terrano.

"POLLUTION! YUCK! That does *not* sound interesting. Why isn't he doing a report about *space*?

That's what he likes to read about!" remarked Erica.

"He did not have a choice this time. His class is studying environmental science, and they were all asked to do research on pollution," replied Erica's Father.

"Oh, then I guess I shouldn't feel disappointed that he won't be reading it to me before he takes it to school. Mark always reads his reports to me if they are about *space* because he knows I want to be an astronaut when I grow up."

"ZOOM! . . . ZOOM! . . . ZOOM! . . . I want to be an astronaut too! I want to go real FAST in a rocket and *zoom* to MARS!" squealed Matthew while jumping up and down on the big chair. He waved the bag of candy through the air like it was a rocket, and before anyone could do anything about it, the pieces of candy soared across the room. Several pieces flew onto Erica's lap.

"Hey what's going on? MATTHEW, did you throw those pieces of candy at me?" shouted Erica.

"They are *not* pieces of candy, they're SHOOTING STARS!"

"MATTHEW, give it back!" demanded Erica.

"Here's the bag, but the candy just went flying around the room. Don't worry, I can pick all of them up and put them back in the bag," whispered Valen as she placed the empty bag on Erica's lap.

Matthew plunged onto Erica's bed, landed across her legs, rolled onto her feet, and started bouncing up and down at the end of the bed.

. . . He was enough of a pest when I could see him, but now that I am blind, he is even more annoying, thought Erica impatiently.

"Why don't you GET OFF MY BED and help Valen pick up the candy!" she yelled.

Erica's father gently patted her shoulder.

"I think we need to get someone home to his *own* bed," he said lightheartedly.

"Good idea!" agreed Erica.

Matthew jumped off the bed and started kicking pieces of candy across the floor.

"Stop being such a PEST! If you want to have any more candy, you have to help me pick it up!" yelled Valen.

Matthew proceeded to pick up pieces of candy and shove them in his pockets.

"*Matthew,* take the pieces of candy *out* of your pockets and put them *in* the bag," said Mrs. Terrano, in a soft but stern voice.

"Do I *HAVE* to?" whined Matthew.

Erica did not hear a direct answer to Matthew's question, but she knew someone must have given him a very serious "do it now" stare because she heard him blurt out, "O . . . KAY! . . . I'M DOING IT!"

While the commotion of Erica's candy bag had everyone's attention, Uncle Garwin put the SOS Receiver back on the table by Erica's bed.

"The SOS Receiver is next to your bed," he said very quietly, making sure Matthew could not hear him. "I am going home now, but I will see you tomorrow— and remember, you are *very brave!*"

"We are sorry we cannot stay longer either, but it *is* getting late," said Mrs. Terrano as she gave Erica a big hug. "We are all very proud of you. We miss you, and we know you will be coming home soon."

Erica's mother hugged her again, and then she held Valen's hand as they walked toward the door together.

"Bye, Erica. I'll hug *MOON* for you," yelled Valen from the doorway. "Your bag of candy is on the bed table!"

Mr. Terrano kissed Erica's forehead.

"Good-bye, Pumpkin," he said affectionately. Then he lifted Matthew onto his shoulders and walked out the door.

"Look at ME, I'm taller than anyone! BYE, ERICA!" yelled Matthew.

. . . Matthew must be up on Dad's shoulders. . . . I wish I could go home with them. I don't want to be alone in the dark again, thought Erica sadly.

She somberly pulled the covers up over her head and almost knocked off her sunglasses.

. . . I forgot I was wearing these. . . . Ha! Matthew really thought they were astronaut glasses. He is probably begging mom for them right now. . . . Well, I put them on to remind myself to have

positive thoughts; sooo . . . think about things you like, thought Erica as she slowly pulled the covers off her head. *Okay, I like having New Moon to hold onto . . .*

Erica hugged New Moon as tightly as she could. The soft, stuffed animal gave her a feeling of security; he was Erica's new protector now that Moon could not be with her in the hospital. Snuggling her face against him, she tried to think of other things that were positive.

. . . I am so happy Matthew told me that he saw Moon in my room, she thought. *. . . Plus, I'm glad that Uncle Garwin came to visit. It was fun eating pizza and listening to his story about the Cosmic Family. . . I liked the way he wrapped my present and . . . hey . . . my present! Awesome! I can listen to the SOS RECEIVER! I can imagine that I am an astronaut who is listening for sounds from SPACE!*

Erica quickly sat up, took off her sunglasses, and set them on the bed table. Then she reached for the headphones and fumbled to put them on. After managing to position them comfortably, she lay back down, snuggled under the covers, and rested her head contentedly on her new, soft pillow.

The fragrance of Erica's favorite fabric softener permeated the pillowcase. She nestled her face into the cushiony pillow and took a deep breath, enjoying the sweet smell. Erica wondered which pillowcase her parents had put on her new, soft pillow. Was it the one with a sun, moon, and stars, the one with clouds, or the one Mark gave her with the planets on it?

. . . I think this is Mark's old pillowcase because it is the oldest one I have and it feels as smooth as this one does. . . . Yes, I'm sure it is, thought Erica as she imagined her head resting in the middle of the solar system. *. . . Now, if I could just HEAR a SOUND coming from the solar system . . .*

Would Erica hear anything? . . . From SPACE? She waited patiently, listening to total silence. It was a silence that offered her much needed comfort and eventually transported her into a deep sleep.

⭐ **Chapter 9 brain teaser:** Why does it make "sense" for Erica to play a guessing game with her candy?

~ Chapter 9 ~

TUESDAY

"*I FOUND* you sleeping with your headphones on when I came to check on you last night," stated the nurse. "I was concerned that you might roll over on them and break them, so I put your headphones on the table next to your bed. . . . Now, here's your breakfast tray, honey. There will be a carton of milk at 12:00, a carton of orange juice at 3:00, and a warm bagel sandwich at 6:00. Please try to eat some of it. You need to keep up your strength."

Erica reluctantly took a bite of her sandwich and was pleasantly surprised.

"Hey, this tastes TERRIFIC!" she said.

"You're in luck. This is *Tuesday*, and they always make egg and cheese on a bagel for breakfast on Tuesday. Enjoy your meal," said the nurse cheerfully, and then she proceeded to hum her way out of the room and down the hall.

When Erica no longer heard the humming, she reached for the SOS Receiver . . . she could hardly wait to try it again. After searching for the "on" button, Erica found that it was already pushed in. She snugly positioned the headphones and contentedly began listening as she savored every bite of her sandwich. It was truly remarkable! Erica was actually eating hospital food alone in the dark and enjoying herself!

After breakfast, Erica held onto New Moon as she continued listening for even the slightest sound to come through the headphones. Sitting alone in darkness and silence, Erica was no longer over-whelmed by her own daunting thoughts. The anger, sadness, and fear that had made her so upset yesterday were the last things on her mind. Now she had *New Moon* and the *SOS Receiver* to keep her company.

Having a bag of candy by her side also helped to make the morning more enjoyable. While Erica began sampling various pieces of candy, she used her senses to play a guessing game as Matthew had suggested. First, she would feel the shape . . . *rectangle* . . . next, the wrapper . . . *aluminum foil* . . . after that, the smell . . . *definitely chocolate.* . . . Then, CHOMP! . . . *Awesome! Caramel and nuts . . . my favorite! What a difference a day makes,* she thought happily.

However, little did Erica know what an amazing difference this day would actually make in her life!

As promised, Uncle Garwin returned later that morning, well prepared to take Erica outside for a picnic. When he came into the hospital room, he found Erica lying in bed with her headphones on. He knew she might not hear him come in, so he placed the bag of warm fried dough that he brought on the table next to her bed.

Erica immediately noticed the tempting smell. She hastily pulled off her headphones and sat up.

"Is someone here? I smell food . . . is it time for lunch already?" she asked curiously.

"It's lunchtime for us!" said Uncle Garwin merrily. "I brought peanut butter and jelly sandwiches made with your grandpa's homemade bread, blueberries from your nana's garden, AND . . . fresh fried dough from the farmer's market on Pultney Square!"

"Yummmmm! I had a good breakfast, but I'm hungry again."

"I certainly am not the least bit surprised. It is almost twelve o'clock. . . . I see you have been listening to the SOS Receiver. Have you heard anything?"

"Not a thing," replied Erica with a disappointed sigh. "I fell asleep listening to it last night, and I listened to it again all morning."

"Hmm . . . well then, let's take the SOS Receiver outside with us for our picnic," suggested Uncle Garwin. "Here, put your sunglasses on and I'll go get a wheelchair."

Erica decided she wanted to take New Moon with her, too. She felt exceptionally proud holding him in her arms while Uncle Garwin pushed her through the hospital halls on their way to the park.

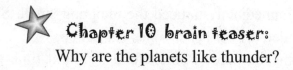

Chapter 10 brain teaser:
Why are the planets like thunder?

~ Chapter 10 ~

A PECULIAR PICNIC

FRESH air in the park was a welcome change from the medicinal aroma that permeated the hospital. Erica enjoyed deep breaths as she felt the warmth of the sun shining on her dark-green sweater and the navy-blue blanket under her. Her uncle was right . . . she did not need to *see* the sun to know that it was there.

Erica placed New Moon in front of her on the blanket. As memories of her last picnic with *Moon* drifted through her thoughts, she unwrapped her sandwich, broke off a tiny piece, and put it next to her silent companion.

. . . *Moon loves peanut butter.* . . . *The last time we were on a picnic, I made a peanut butter and jelly sandwich for him and cut it into little squares,* thought Erica dreamily. . . . *Moon sat next to me on the blanket eating his pieces of sandwich, but he never even tried to eat my food.* . . . *He is such a good dog, and I really miss him.* . . . *Hey, I wonder if he's going to figure out that I can't see him and start doing things he's not supposed to do?*

Erica enjoyed every morsel of her meal. Slowly biting around the edges of the thick, homemade bread, she formed the sandwich into a circle . . . after which she carefully gnawed her sandwich into smaller circles, contently nibbling until the last circle was her last bite. Then, she smoothed her hands across the warm blanket and picked up the bag of blueberries. Counting each berry as she ate it, Erica marveled at the luscious burst of flavor every time she squished one in her mouth. Finally, Erica started eating dessert, allowing each small bite of sugar and dough to dissolve on her tongue before she took another bite.

Anxious to examine the receiver, Uncle Garwin finished eating long before Erica finished savoring her dessert. He disconnected the headphones, pushed "play," and listened attentively . . . not a sound.

"You said you fell asleep listening to the receiver last night. Was it on *all* night?" he asked.

"Well, it must have been because the 'on' button was pushed in when I started to use it this morning, replied Erica. "Is that a problem?"

"No, I'll just change the batteries. Maybe that's why you haven't heard anything on the receiver today."

While Uncle Garwin was replacing the batteries, a red slot on the side of the receiver caught his attention. "I think I see the reason why you haven't heard anything through the headphones. The 'record' button is on. You wouldn't be able to hear *anything* at that setting," he explained.

"But I'm sure I only pushed the 'on' button, replied Erica defensively. "I never touched any other buttons!"

"It is certainly a possibility that Matthew switched the setting to 'record' when he was playing with it yesterday," suggested Uncle Garwin. "It's a small button on the side, but knowing Matthew, he probably found it. I didn't check the setting when I took it from him yesterday, and I didn't check it before I put it next to your bed last night either."

"WHAT! MATTHEW was playing with my SOS Receiver?" yelled Erica angrily. "He's such a PEST! He really messed everything up! . . . Now I've been listening all this time on the wrong setting!"

"I know it *is* frustrating, but no harm done. I'll push 'play' and see if any sounds were recorded," said Uncle Garwin.

Erica waited patiently, which was extremely difficult because she was very excited. There was a chance that the SOS Receiver had recorded some sounds from space. She would be happy to hear just *one* . . . from SPACE! It would be incredible!

Uncle Garwin sat right next to Erica on the blanket and turned the volume on the receiver all the way up to "high."

"Let's see if there were any sounds recorded," he said with a cheerful grin.

Erica and her uncle listened intently, assuming they might miss a sound if they did not pay close attention. They waited . . . and waited . . . and waited . . . total silence. The only sound they heard was the clicking squeal of a squirrel in a nearby tree, begging for the morsel of Erica's sandwich lying by New Moon.

Then *suddenly*, and much to their surprise, they heard a loud, rumbling sound. Like the loudest earsplitting thunder you could possibly imagine, the powerful rumbling roared through their ears and echoed throughout the park. However, as they listened, they realized the rumbling was more than a resounding noise. The rumbling was a deep, strong voice booming out the words . . .

"EARTH IS CRYING!"

Uncle Garwin pushed the "stop" button.

"DID YOU HEAR THAT?" he yelled.

"I *HEARD* it alright! *WHO* was it? *WHAT* was it? Did it say *EARTH IS CRYING?*" responded Erica, yelling just as loudly as her uncle did.

"That's what I thought I heard too—and the source function has spelled out the name *VENUS!*" answered Uncle Garwin in complete astonishment.

He turned the volume down and pushed the "play" button . . . again the voice rumbled through the machine.

"MARS, CAN YOU HEAR ME? . . . EARTH IS CRYING!"

Once again the receiver's source function spelled out the name *VENUS*.

Uncle Garwin stopped the machine and stood up abruptly. He began pacing back and forth, as jumbled thoughts transformed into a rambling attempt to explain the peculiar response of his invention.

"I *never* expected . . . actual *voices* . . . and of a PLANET? This is *incredible!* It's *phenomenally* incredible! . . . I just cannot believe this . . . cannot believe . . . just cannot . . ."

"IS IT REAL?" interrupted Erica loudly. "You aren't TRICKING me, are you?"

"No, Pumpkin, I'm *not* tricking you . . . and since I made this receiver, I don't see how anyone could be tricking *me* either!"

"DO YOU THINK THERE'S MORE? LET'S LISTEN FOR MORE!" shouted Erica, unable to contain her excitement.

Uncle Garwin quickly pushed the "on" button and another thunderous voice burst through the receiver.

"YES, I KNOW . . ."

"WHO'S THAT?" yelled Erica.

"The source function has spelled out the name . . . *MARS!* . . . This is UNPRECEDENTED!" exclaimed Uncle Garwin.

"HEY," shouted Erica, "THERE'S MORE!"

They were both motionless statues, listening with incomprehensible amazement as thunderous voices continued to bellow through the SOS Receiver. . . .

"WHY IS SHE CRYING?"

"I 'M NOT SURE!"

"WHAT'S WRONG WITH HER? ... PLEASE TELL US! "

"Hey, *what's* going on? *Who's* talking?" asked Erica anxiously.

"Well, so far, I see the names *MARS, VENUS* and *MERCURY* on the source function," said Uncle Garwin.

"I *don't* believe it!" replied Erica skeptically.

"I can't believe it *myself*, but that's what it says!"

"I wish I could *see* the source functions. Besides, I'm kind of getting confused," admitted Erica.

"That's *completely* understandable, I'm quite confused myself! Now, I know you are excited to hear more, but I'm going to take this to my lab and . . ."

"YOU'RE WHAT?" gasped Erica as she lunged out of the wheelchair, clumsily tripping over New Moon.

Uncle Garwin quickly stepped forward and caught her just in time to avoid another accident. "Careful now, Erica," he said, leading her back toward the wheelchair.

"BUT . . ." Erica's mind went blank. After all, it was difficult enough to argue with Uncle Garwin when it came to matters that required urgent investigation of inventions and discoveries *if* you had a *clear* mind. Unfortunately, *Erica's* mind was cluttered with sudden confusion and disappointment, and she could not manage to think fast enough to convince her uncle to reconsider.

"I understand you want to hear more, nonetheless, I *must* take this to my lab," he insisted while gently placing his stunned niece in the wheelchair. Then, as soon as Erica was safely seated, Uncle Garwin rushed around cleaning up leftovers from the picnic.

After quickly throwing everything into a thoroughly crumpled paper bag, he grabbed the blanket, shoved it into the bag as well, and plopped it on Erica's lap. Then, hastily assuming that he had collected everything from the picnic, he directed the wheelchair toward the hospital. However, in his rush, Uncle Garwin never noticed the green sweater Erica had tossed on the grass while she was eating.

"I'm going to put the disc in my computer and make a printed copy with the source functions on it. Then, I'll bring it back and read it to you, so you can understand who is talking," stated Uncle Garwin while carefully pushing Erica across the bumpy grass, and then up the sidewalk toward the hospital.

"I'm also going to make a copy of the voices on another disc—so you can listen to it as many times as you want to . . . I promise!" said Uncle Garwin firmly.

Before Erica had a chance to protest, she was back in the hospital bed, and her very astounded uncle hurried off to his laboratory.

⭐ **Chapter 11 brain teaser:** What do you call someone who is awesome and lives far away?

~ Chapter 11 ~

THE SOS TRANSCRIPTS

WHEN Uncle Garwin returned later that day, his excitement exploded throughout the hospital room like fireworks at a carnival. Although Erica was not able to see her uncle, she listened to him talk on and on and on about the SOS Receiver and realized how overwhelmed he was with his new discovery. She could not remember a time when a grown-up's voice contained quite as much excitement as her uncle's did.

"After I put the disc into my computer to print out the recordings from the SOS Receiver, I got more than I thought I would!" exclaimed Uncle Garwin, pacing back and forth across the room and flipping through a stack of papers.

"Not only did it print out what the planets are saying, it printed it out like a *story*, with *dialogue* and *narration*. I named it the *SOS TRANSCRIPTS*. This is so incredible! It is certainly beyond my wildest scientific imagination! AUGH! . . . OUCH!" he yelled.

Erica heard a loud thump.

"What *happened*? Are you okay?" she asked.

Uncle Garwin was sprawled across the big chair and the SOS Transcripts were all over the floor.

"No problem . . . just have to remember to watch out for this BIG chair in here!" he replied while rubbing his sore shin with one hand and hastily gathering papers with the other.

"As I was saying, I have organized the SOS Transcripts into several chapters. I named the first chapter *EARTH IS CRYING*. . . . Listen to this, Erica, we have discovered something monumental! Chapter One . . . *Earth is Crying*," said Uncle Garwin, and he started reading the SOS Transcripts to his curious niece.

THE SOS TRANSCRIPTS

Ø...Ø...Ø...

EARTH IS CRYING! MARS, can you hear me? ... EARTH IS CRYING!

"I know," sighed Mars.
"WHY is she crying?" asked Venus.
"I'm not sure," answered Mars.
"WHAT'S WRONG WITH HER?" asked Venus more persistently.

Please tell us! PLEASE! Come on, tell us!

I don't really know, but she said something about not being able to take care of her humans.

"HUMANS! What are HUMANS?" asked Mercury.

"Yes, what are humans?" added Venus. "I overheard Mom and Dad mention Earth's humans once, but I wasn't sure what they were talking about. And whatever the humans are, I didn't know Earth had to *take care* of them."

"I'm not sure what humans are either . . . and I didn't realize they were so important to her. I'd ask Mom and Dad about this, but Earth wants me to keep it a SECRET, so we'd better make sure Earth doesn't know we're talking about her," said Mars.

"Well, I'm pretty sure she won't know we're talking about her because Earth just passed by me on her way to the other side of Great-Grandmother Sun, so I think we'll be okay for awhile," said Venus.

"Great-Grandma's solar storm will also help block out our conversation. And Mom and Dad are on the other side of our great-grandmother, too, so they won't know we're talking about Earth either," replied Mars.

"I'LL LET YOU KNOW IF I SEE THEM COMING!" yelled Mercury excitedly.

"OKAY! You don't have to be so loud! Just keep watch for us . . . Mars and I have to figure out a way to help Earth. . . . But I'm not sure we can help Earth if we don't know what humans are," said Venus.

"I know what to do!" interrupted Mercury. "We can ask Uncle Pluto. He's really *FAR OUT!* And he can keep a secret too! I know because once I stayed up late to watch Haley's Comet and he never told Mom and Dad about it!"

"NO, we can't! I PROMISED!" insisted Mars.

"Mercury does have a point," admitted Venus. "We should tell Uncle Pluto."

"Come on, Mars. Let's tell Uncle Pluto!" begged Mercury.

Mars felt confused. He did not want to break his promise, but he was worried about Earth. What were these "humans" Earth was talking about—and why was she crying about not being able to take care of them?

"Listen, Mars, you know we can't take care of this problem ourselves—we just don't know enough about it. We really should talk to Uncle Pluto. He might be able to help."

"VENUS IS RIGHT . . . Uncle Pluto can help! PLEASE, Mars! Can we tell him? PLEASE!" pleaded Mercury.

"Maybe Uncle Pluto *could* help, but . . ."

Ø . . . Ø . . . Ø . . .

Uncle Garwin stopped reading for a moment and glanced at the door.

"It looks like your dinner is here," he said.

"I was so interested in listening to the SOS Transcripts, I wasn't paying attention to anything else. I didn't even hear someone come into the room, but . . ."

As the nurse removed the lid from Erica's dinner plate, Erica got a strong whiff of a very unpleasant odor.

"YUCK! What is that s*mell*? I don't think I'm very hungry!" she grumbled.

"I realize that you had quite a filling lunch, but try to eat some of this meal if you can," said Uncle Garwin.

"UGH! It smells like rotten garbage! I think somebody made a mistake and put this stuff on my plate instead of putting it in a compost pile!"

Uncle Garwin cracked up laughing.

"Oh, come on . . . it can't be *that* bad!"

He tasted a spoonful, reluctantly swallowed it, and then drank a big gulp of his cold coffee.

"They brought you chocolate milk, so why don't you just drink your milk and eat the roll—how does that sound?" he said.

"That sounds okay to me," agreed Erica.

"So what do you think about the transcripts so far?" asked Uncle Garwin.

A big grin spread across Erica's face.

"They're *astronomical! Now* I know why you banged into the chair when you were telling me about them! I can't believe this is really happening!" she said enthusiastically. "I love learning about space, but I never thought I'd ever actually *listen* to the planets *talking* to each other. Uncle Garwin, you're a GENIUS! You recorded the planets talking!"

Erica's uncle chuckled rather proudly.

"Indeed, it appears as though I did, but don't call me a genius yet! We have come a long way from waiting to hear some sounds come through the SOS Receiver to having these SOS Transcripts, but I am still not sure exactly how this is happening. I must say, it is definitely a mystery that has brought my curiosity to a peak as high as Mount Everest, and I am determined to find a factual explanation for our discovery," he replied.

"This is *so* exciting! The PLANETS are talking through the SOS Receiver, AND a story about them is coming through your computer. . . . Plus I wonder why Earth is crying. Do Mars, Venus, and Mercury talk to Uncle Pluto about it?" asked Erica.

"Yes, indeed, they most certainly do!"

"I can't wait to hear it! Will you read it to me right now?"

⭐ **Chapter 12 brain teaser:** Who has more children than any other mother in the world?

~ Chapter 12 ~

HUMANS

WHILE Erica munched on a roll and sipped chocolate milk, her uncle settled into the big chair.

"Chapter Two . . . *Humans*," said Uncle Garwin, and then he began to read the chapter to his niece.

Ø . . . Ø . . . Ø . . .

As far as Mercury was concerned, "maybe" meant "yes." Before Mars had a chance to stop him it was too late. Mercury was already trying to tell Uncle Pluto his version of the problem.

HUMANS

"Uncle Pluto! Uncle Pluto!" shouted Mercury. "Earth has humans, and she won't tell mom and dad!"

"What's going on here?" questioned Uncle Pluto.

"I'm not sure. Earth is crying—and she said something about not being able to take care of her humans. . . . We want to help her, but we don't even know what humans are," explained Mars.

"Do you know what they are?" asked Venus.

"How much is a BILLION?" interrupted Mercury.

"A billion is a thousand million," answered Uncle Pluto.

"Well, how much is a million?"

"A million is a thousand thousand."

"Well, how much is . . ."

"It's a lot!" said Venus impatiently. "Now, let's finish listening to what Uncle Pluto has to say about these humans."

"Ah, yes . . . humans can stand and move around on Earth because they have legs and feet. They can also carry things that Earth gives them because they have arms and hands," continued Uncle Pluto. "They get everything they need to survive from your sister, Earth. She takes care of them and loves them as much as your mother loves you, so they call her *Mother Earth.*"

"How come those six billion humans aren't zooming around in space like us? How come they all stay on Earth?" asked Mercury.

"GRAVITY keeps them from floating out into space," replied Uncle Pluto.

"What's 'GRAVY'?" asked Mercury.

"It's *GRAV-I-TY!* Pay attention," snapped Venus.

"GRAVITY is a universal force that attracts

things to each other. The gravity of Great-Grandmother Sun keeps us from flying off into other parts of our Milky Way Galaxy, and Earth's gravity keeps the humans from floating into space," explained Uncle Pluto.

"That's *not* fair! How come she gets a lot of humans and we don't have any?" complained Mercury. "Don't we have that grav . . . uh . . . that 'gravy stuff' too?" he asked.

Uncle Pluto had to give that question a little thought. "Well . . . yes, we all do have *some* gravity—but . . ."

"Then why don't we have humans?" asked Venus.

"Hey, that's what I want to know! WHY don't we have humans? I want some! I really want some!" begged Mercury.

Ø . . . Ø . . . Ø . . .

"Mercury sure is a PEST!" commented Erica. "I know this may sound strange, but Mercury reminds me of my little brother. . . . Now that I think about it, I am really glad Matthew didn't break the SOS Receiver when he was playing around with it."

"I must say, it actually turned out to be lucky for us that Matthew *did* push the 'record' knob. Now we have the planets recorded on the SOS Receiver and I can read the SOS Transcripts to you."

"I guess it did work out that way, didn't it?"

"Sometimes, no matter how well we plan things, they are just meant to happen another way," replied Uncle Garwin.

Erica thought about that for a minute . . . she was starting to detect even more of a similarity between the planets and her family.

. . . Meant to happen in a very UNUSUAL way, she thought. *. . . I have a little brother who's a pest, just like Mercury. I also have an older brother and a younger sister, just like Earth does . . . and I had a secret that was making me cry, just like Earth does . . . maybe . . .*

Uncle Garwin noticed that Erica seemed unusually quiet. "Are you tired? . . . Would you like to rest for awhile?" he asked softly.

"No thanks. I really want to hear some more. I want to find out if Uncle Pluto knows why Mars, Venus and Mercury don't have humans," replied Erica.

"Well, you will find out what he has to say about that in the very next sentence of this chapter," said Uncle Garwin, and then he continued reading Chapter Two of the SOS Transcripts . . .

Ø . . . Ø . . . Ø . . .

"Uh, hmm . . . I really don't know why Earth is the only planet in our family who has humans," admitted Uncle Pluto. "Did you ask your parents?"

"Earth doesn't want me to say anything to them about this," answered Mars. "We can't tell them. It's supposed to be a *secret!*"

"But this must be serious if Earth is crying. I think we should at least tell your grandparents about this," said Uncle Pluto.

"I agree . . . maybe our grandparents could tell us if WE can take care of Earth's humans until she gets better," added Venus, hopeful that she might have a chance to take care of some humans. After all, Mars has two moons— and Earth has one moon and six billion humans. If she could not have a moon, at least she might be able to have some humans.

"I don't know. . ." Mars was reluctant to share the secret with anyone else. He already felt as if he should not have told Uncle Pluto.

"It's the responsible thing to do," said Uncle Pluto. "Earth could have a serious problem and need help."

"I know you're right. If there really is a chance we can help Earth, then we have to try," said Mars.

"Yippee!" bellowed Mercury. "Let's go ask Grandma and Grandpa!"

Mars directed an irritated glance toward Mercury. "Shhh . . . it's a *secret!*" he whispered.

"Grandma! Grandpa! Earth has humans! We want some and we don't know why we can't have some," blurted Mercury.

"*GARGANTUAN GALAXIES!* What is all the commotion about?" asked Grandfather Neptune.

"Earth is crying, and she told me that she is worried about not being able to take care of her humans," explained Mars. "She wanted me to keep it a secret, but if she is crying, she may have a big problem. We want to help her, but we don't even know why Earth is the only one in our family who has humans. Do you know why?"

"Yes, I do."

"Can you please tell us," asked Venus. "I would like to know if I could take care of her humans while she's sick."

"Please tell us!" begged Mercury. "I really want to know because I want some humans, too! It would be COOL! I could *zoom* them around Great-Grandmother Sun quicker than any other planet!"

"Maybe if we find a way to help Earth, she won't be angry at me for sharing her *secret*," added Mars.

"Hey! I have *EXCITEMENT!*" interrupted Mercury.

"It's *EN-VI-RON-MENT!*" chuckled Grandfather Neptune.

"What's that?" asked Mercury

"I don't know what *environment* is either," said Venus.

"Neither do I," admitted Mars. . . .

⭐ **Chapter 13 brain teaser:**

Why is Erica's mind like a rotating planet?

~ Chapter 13 ~

THE BLACK HOLE

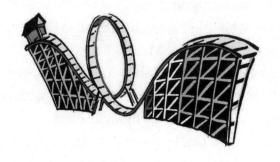

AS ERICA listened to the planets talking about *Earth's secret*, her thoughts continually revolved around her own family . . . her accident . . . her secret . . .

. . . Maybe Mark wasn't going to tell anyone the secret about my accident, just like Mars when he tried not to tell Earth's secret. . . . Maybe Valen and Matthew bugged him about it, just like Venus and

VOICES IN THE DARK

Mercury bugged Mars. . . . Maybe Matthew was the "tattletale," she mused.

"Who told you about my accident?" asked Erica.

"Actually, Matthew was the one who told me."

"Oh, I *knew* it! I just *knew* it!" yelled Erica sharply.

"Well, now, no need to get angry," said Uncle Garwin. "Valen heard you crying up in the attic, and she asked Mark if he knew what was wrong. So Mark told Valen about the accident, and then she tried to convince him to tell one of the adults in the family about it. . . . Matthew overheard their conversation and told me what was going on."

"Then, who told Nana and Grandpa?"

"After I talked to Mark about your accident, he realized that you probably needed to get to the hospital, so he decided to tell your grandparents."

Whoa! Stop the ride! thought Erica.

Listening to Uncle Garwin's answer felt like the first time she went on the *Black Hole* at Galaxy Trek Amusement Park. She had wanted to find out what the ride was like, but after she went on it, UGH . . . she had felt quite woozy, just like she did now.

Erica's mind was spinning. The SOS Transcripts were getting *creepy*. The planets in the SOS Transcripts seemed too much like her real family. It was as if someone were trying to get a message to her, especially the part about Mark and her accident!

Furthermore, was it just a "coincidence" that the Cosmic Family from her uncle's story was so much like the planets in the SOS Transcripts *and* like her family also?

"Are you okay?" asked Uncle Garwin.

"Huh? . . . Oh, yeah, I'm okay . . . I was just day-dreaming. Well, I mean . . . I was wondering about something. All this stuff in the SOS Transcripts, is it *really* coming from the SOS Receiver? . . . It's not a big trick, is it?" asked Erica suspiciously.

"Well, if it *is* a trick, *I* am not doing it!" insisted Uncle Garwin.

"It's just that *you* made up the story about the Cosmic Family, and the planets from your story are a lot like the planets in the SOS Transcripts. Plus, they *both* are a lot like our family," explained Erica. She did not want to tell her uncle that it seemed so weird it was making her head spin. That certainly was not worth the chance that he might stop reading the transcripts to her.

. . . Besides, I am a brave person, she told herself. *I got back on the Black Hole a lot of times after the first time I got so dizzy. . . . If I got used to that crazy ride, I can get used to this weird stuff about the planets and my family.*

"I admit it," replied Uncle Garwin. "When I told the story about the Cosmic Family, I *did* give the planets character traits that are like people in our family, and I *did* make the SOS Receiver—but that is where my part in this mystery ends. I am completely baffled by the planets' voices coming from the SOS Receiver *and* the story form of the SOS Transcripts."

"I know one thing . . . listening to the SOS Transcripts is making me feel terrible about calling Mark a 'tattletale.' Now I know that Matthew was the pesky little 'tattletale,' and Mark was just trying to be helpful," said Erica regretfully.

"Well, you know Matthew. It was just his way of trying to be a part of things. He knew Mark and Valen were worried about you, and you *also* know how important it was to get you to the hospital as soon as possible."

"I guess sometimes we shouldn't keep a secret, even if we promised we would," admitted Erica.

"Especially if the secret involves someone who has been hurt *or* is in danger of getting hurt, and you need to get help for them," added Uncle Garwin.

"I hope Mark isn't mad at me . . . and I hope he doesn't think I'm still mad at him!"

Erica's uncle leaned over and whispered into her ear.

"What a coincidence . . . this is your chance to find out; your grandparents and Mark are here," he said.

⭐ **Chapter 14 brain teaser:** Why would someone from the Terrano family be named "Earth's choice"?

~ Chapter 14 ~

A SPECIAL GIFT

"*I HAVE* something for you." Mark handed Erica a beautiful bouquet of flowers. "Mom let me cut some of her roses, and Valen gave me snap dragons from her flower garden. I wrapped the stems in wet paper towels and covered them with aluminum foil so you can hold onto them in bed if you want to. The bouquet has ten stems of flowers. There is one from everyone in the family, because we all miss you. There is even one from *Moon*—he misses you, too."

Mark's thoughtful gift touched Erica's heart, and she realized just how kind her brother really is.

. . . I'm lucky to have such a nice brother! I never should have gotten so mad at him. I should apologize, but I am afraid to. I don't know why . . . but I am just afraid. . . . NO . . . NO, she reminded herself *. . . I am NOT AFRAID . . . I am BRAVE. I can do this!*

Erica breathed in the sweet scent of the flowers, and their fragrance was like a tonic for bravery. As she clung tightly to New Moon and kept the flowers close to her face, tears began to roll down her cheeks. However, she was not ashamed. In fact, Erica did something very brave.

With everyone's attention quietly directed at the teary-eyed patient who was clutching her precious gifts, the silence was broken by her humble voice.

"Mark, I am s-so s-sorry." Erica was sobbing her heart out now, but she did not care. She kept right on apologizing through the sobs. "I sh-should-d-dn't have g-gotten s-so m-mad and called you a t-tat-tle . . . t-tale."

"It's okay," answered Mark.

He gave Erica and New Moon a huge hug.

"I am just glad you are going to be okay," he said sympathetically.

While sitting comfortably in the big chair, Grandpa chuckled loudly.

"Well, *JUMPIN' JUNEBUGS!* What a touching moment. I wish we brought the camera!" he bellowed.

A SPECIAL GIFT

"I am pleased that you two kids finally got a chance to talk to each other and settle things between yourselves. Your grandpa and I are very proud of you," added Nana, handing Erica a tissue.

"Thanks, Nana . . . and thanks for bringing Mark to visit me," replied Erica as she wiped the remaining tears from her eyes.

"You are *very* welcome, but it was Mark's idea. He was deeply disappointed that he had to stay and work on his homework last night instead of coming to see you."

"So, how did your science report turn out?" asked Erica.

"It took me a long time because there is so much information about pollution, but I think it turned out okay. I really learned a lot too."

Erica slipped her sunglasses on. Then, trying to conceal a large grin, she held the bouquet in front of her face and pretended to smell the flowers.

"I'd rather find out a lot of information about the solar system—wouldn't you, Uncle Garwin?"

"Well I'm sure Mark found out some very interesting information about pollution," replied Uncle Garwin.

"*You* know what I mean!" insisted Erica. She burst into laughter as her sunglasses bobbed up and down behind scarlet roses and ivory snapdragons.

It was a comical sight, and Mark could not resist the chance to say something about it. After all, now that things were settled between them, it was his brotherly responsibility to resume teasing her again.

"*Radical* sunglasses, Erica, but it happens to be cloudy inside the hospital today. . . . And, *what* is so funny? Is the scent of those flowers making you goofy or something? . . . Oh, I get it! Did I miss one of Uncle Garwin's solar system stories?" he asked.

Erica dropped the bouquet of flowers on her lap and giggled.

"YOU SURE DID!" she shouted.

"Well, I have an unusual story to tell you, too," stated Mark.

"What is it about?" asked Erica.

"I know you are probably not interested in learning about pollution, but while I was doing research for my report on the internet, I found something that really *jolts*. It seems there is a folktale about our last name."

"There is?"

"Yes. . . . I was skimming through stories from different websites about pollution caused by fires, and I came across this folktale. After I read it, I was in a hurry so I only printed out the last page—but I think I remember enough about it to tell the story to you. Would you like to hear it?"

"SURE I WOULD!"

"I would also like to hear it," added Nana.

"Okay," said Mark, "it goes something like this. . . . A long time ago there was this terrible fire on an island in the Mediterranean Sea. It killed many animals that the people used for food and ruined a lot of their grape vineyards and olive orchards. It also burned all of the barley on the island.

"Without the barley, the people could not trade with other islands for food. The fishermen caught fish every day, and everyone shared the food that was left on the island—but the people were still hungry.

"Then there was this girl, I think her name was *Areeka.* Anyway, she led her uncle and brother on a dangerous journey to find barley seeds, and they say she was protected by a wolf and guided by a mysterious light. . . . When they came back with the barley seeds, the people on the island let the girl and her family plant the seeds."

Mark reached into his pocket, pulled out a crumpled piece of paper and started reading the rest of the story. . . .

Planting barley seeds in the earth was a privileged custom in their culture. The people believed the mysterious life force in Earth's soil that transforms seeds into plants only allowed seeds to germinate if the seeds were sowed by someone whose heart was filled with love for Earth.

The barley crop yielded so much barley the people had enough seeds to grow more crops and trade for food. They came to believe that the girl and her family were very special and must have been chosen by Earth's life force to restore barley crops on the island. As a result, Areeka's family was honored with the name *Terra Annuo*. *Terra* means *earth*, as in *soil*, and *Annuo* means *choice*. . . . Then, as time went by, the name was shortened to *Terrano*.

"BIZZARO!" yelled Erica. "I never knew our family name had such an important meaning! This is so awesome!"

"BIZZARO? Where did you learn *that* word?" asked Nana curiously.

"I've heard it somewhere before. I'm not really sure what it means, but I just gave it my own meaning."

"And what might that be?" smiled Nana.

"It means . . . *oh, that's totally bizarre!*" replied Erica proudly.

"*Bizzaro! Peculiaro! Extraordinaro!*" laughed Grandpa. "I agree with Erica, this story about our last name is bizarre."

"I thought it was very interesting," added Nana, "and I have to say the Terrano's do have a *special gift* for planting seeds and taking care of their gardens."

Grandpa snickered.

"So, the Terrano's love to sow seeds in Earth's *earth*!" he said jokingly.

"Not *all* of us like to sow seeds. . . . I guess Uncle Garwin, Mark and I are the odd ones who love space and the planets instead of *dirt!*" replied Erica with a tang of sarcasm.

Grinning at Grandpa, Mark laughed.

"I like *eating* food from the garden! Does that count?" he asked jokingly.

Still relaxing in the big chair, Grandpa chuckled loudly again.

"I'm with you, Mark. The *food* is my favorite part too!" he said.

"Well, I am certainly curious to read that folktale sometime soon," stated Uncle Garwin.

"I can pull up the website I found it on and make a copy for you. If it's not too late when I get home I can do it today," said Mark. Then he took a quick glance at the clock.

"OH, MY GOSH! WE HAVE TO GO!" he yelled.

"We do?" asked Grandpa. "What for?"

Nana stared at Grandpa through her thick bifocals and pointed at Mark.

"*WIGGLIN' WORMS!* You are right! Well, it must have slipped my mind. I guess we *do* have to go!"

Grandpa reluctantly pulled himself out of the big chair. He strode over to Erica and wiggled his fingers like little worms squirming around on Erica's chin, and then he gently squeezed the tip of her nose.

"Good-bye, my little *pulchritudinous* pumpkin!" he said affectionately.

"We love you, honey," said Nana as she gave Erica a big hug and kissed her forehead.

"What's going on? Why are you in such a hurry?" asked Erica inquisitively.

"It's a SURPRISE!" answered Mark. Talk to you later, Sis!"

⭐ **Chapter 15 brain teaser:** Why does Erica need to know that "Little Red Puppies Smell Trouble"?

~ *Chapter 15* ~

THE COSMIC COMMUNICATOR

"*I AM* pleased you had a chance to talk with Mark and that everything is okay between the two of you," said Uncle Garwin.

He had been genuinely concerned there might be a permanent rift between Erica and Mark because of the accident. Mark was already in the middle of his teens. Many boys his age do not want to be bothered with a younger sister, but Mark and Erica had always been good friends, and they both had quite a bit in common with Uncle Garwin. The three of them often spent time together looking through their uncle's telescope or hiking through the forest behind their grandparents' house.

"I'm glad, too," agreed Erica, "but I wanted him to stay longer so I could tell him all about the SOS Transcripts and how much the planets remind me of our family."

"I know you did, but I don't think we should mention this to anyone yet."

"WHY NOT?" asked Erica disappointedly.

"Because I want to be sure I know what I am talking about before I try to explain it to anyone else," he replied.

Erica was sure her Uncle was walking around the room while he was talking to her because his voice seemed to be coming from different directions. "I can tell you are pacing because I have to keep turning my head in different directions to hear you. Are you watching where you are going this time? I don't want you to fall and hit your head like I did!"

"No problem, I am not looking at the transcripts and pacing, I am *just* pacing," replied Uncle Garwin. He turned his head to look at Erica and continued walking . . .

"But thanks for . . . **UGH!**"

BANG! CRASH! SPLATTER! SPLASH!
"OH, I AM SO SORRY, MISS!"

The nurse who had just entered the room with Erica's medication was rubbing her forehead, the metal tray and pills were on the floor, and apple juice decorated the front of the nurse's uniform.

"WHAT HAPPENED?" asked Erica loudly. "ARE YOU OKAY?"

"I . . . I am fine; we just had a little accident. I am sure the nurse can get you more juice and pills. . . . OH, and . . . uh . . . get a clean uniform," mumbled Uncle Garwin. He was stooped down on the floor attempting to clean up the mess with one hand and holding the side of his head with his other hand.

Erica had to stifle a hardy laugh. She was not quite sure why, but the vision she imagined of a tray flinging across the room and juice spilling all over the nurse as she collided with her uncle seemed very comical to her.

Still holding his head, Uncle Garwin sat at the end of Erica's bed and continued talking.

"The problem is . . . I do not have a scientific explanation for the voices of the planets that were recorded on the SOS Receiver, *and* I do not know why my computer printed the recorded voices in the form of a story with dialogue and expressions. . . .

"Quite frankly, I *have* noticed the similarities between the planets and our family, too," continued

Uncle Garwin. "Nonetheless, I have been so curious about *how* the SOS Receiver is working and the unusual *form* of the SOS Transcripts, I actually have not given the character similarities very much attention."

"Maybe it's just our imagination," suggested Erica.

"Well, if the family similarities are only our imagination, then there surely is nothing wrong with that! Incredible inventions are usually made by people with creative imaginations."

"Like your SOS Receiver—THAT'S an incredible invention! . . . And, do you know what?"

"What?" replied Uncle Garwin.

"I know *SOS* stands for *Sounds Of Space,* but it could also mean *Save Our Sister.* . . . We can pretend we are two scientists with a special mission, and we can pretend we are trying to find out why Mars, Venus, and Mercury have to save their sister!" said Erica eagerly.

"Indeed, we *are* two scientists with a special mission. We really will find out why Earth is crying— AND why the planets' voices are mysteriously channeling through the SOS Receiver and then printing out as a story through my computer. We can call our mission the *SOS Project.* . . . It could be the discovery of the century! In fact, we can get started right now. Here, I brought you some new technology

for our project. . . . I know it isn't as incredible as the
SOS Receiver, but I *promise* you can *keep* this one!"
said Uncle Garwin as he handed his niece her new gift.

"It feels like a cell phone," said Erica. "Oh, except
for these big buttons on the top. What are they for?
There's a big button on the bottom too. What is this
thing anyway?"

"I call it the *Cosmic Communicator*," said Uncle
Garwin. "It used to be just a cell phone, but I programmed it to do other things as well. Now you can
use it as a cell phone, you can use it to listen to a disc
of the SOS Transcripts, *or* you can talk into it and it
will record everything you say and then play it back
again. . . . I have been utilizing it at night to record my
observations when I am using the telescope because it
is so easy to use in the dark."

"Wow! How do I do all of those things?" asked
Erica inquisitively.

Uncle Garwin took the phone in one hand and
placed Erica's fingers on the top buttons.

"There are four large buttons on top . . . here,
spread your fingers apart like you are playing the piano
—you are good at that," he said. "The first button is
listen, which allows you to listen to the SOS
Transcripts. . . . The second button is *record* . . . the
third button is *play* . . . and the fourth button is *stop*. . . .
You can use your thumb for the button on the bottom,
which is *talk*. The *talk* button allows you to

use this as a cell phone. The Cosmic Communicator is 'voice activated,' so you can talk to me, your parents, your grandparents, or Mark on their cell phones just by saying their name after you push the button. You do not have to worry about using the buttons in the middle unless you want to call someone else," explained Uncle Garwin.

"What an AWESOME gift!" replied Erica excitedly.

"Now, try it yourself . . . can you find the five different buttons with your fingers?"

"I can find the different buttons, but I don't know if I can remember what the buttons are for," replied Erica.

"I thought of that, so I made up a funny mnemonic device to help you remember."

"You mean like this . . . *Maybe Valen's Eating More Jumbo Sourballs Under Nana's Porch!* Isn't it funny? Remember the time when Valen was only about three years old and we couldn't find her anywhere?" asked Erica.

"Ah . . . and then you found her under Nana's porch eating a big bag of sourballs. Hah! That is funny!" answered Uncle Garwin. "However, I am quite curious . . . what does that *mnemonic* device help you remember?"

"It helps me remember the planets in order from the sun—like this . . . *Mercury, Venus, Earth, Mars, Jupiter, Saturn, Uranus, Neptune, Pluto,*" said Erica proudly.

"*Exemplary* example, Erica!"

"Thanks. . . . What, uh . . . new . . . monic device did you make up for me to use with the Cosmic Communicator?"

Uncle Garwin chuckled.

"LITTLE RED PUPPIES SMELL TROUBLE!" he answered cheerfully.

"That's funny too," laughed Erica. "I can remember that . . . *Little Red Puppies Smell Trouble.* . . . *L* is for *Listen* . . . *R* is for *Record.* . . *P* is for *Play* . . . *S* is for *Stop* . . . and *T* is for *Talk.*"

"PERFECT! You've got it!" said Uncle Garwin. "I brought a disc that contains copies of *Earth is Crying* and *Humans.* I also brought a set of headphones to use with your Cosmic Communicator. So now you can lie back and hold New Moon while you listen to the planets talking."

Erica sat up and hugged New Moon as tightly as she could.

"THIS IS GOING TO BE SO MUCH FUN!" she yelled happily.

Now that she had smoothed things over with Mark and was revved up to make the "discovery of the century" with her uncle, the weirdness of similarities between her family and the planets was no longer a baffling intrusion to her brain. It had become a mystery to be solved . . . a challenge to pursue! She was ready to "ride the *black hole*" again!

"I also brought a blank disc. Maybe you will think of something to record on it after I read Chapter Three of the SOS Transcripts."

"Do you have it with you?" asked Erica eagerly.

"Sure do. I have the transcripts with me, and I recorded this chapter on the other disc that contains the first two chapters. AND, IT IS EXTRAORDINARY! In fact, it's so extraordinary, I named it *Extraordinary Environments*," replied Uncle Garwin.

⭐ **Chapter 16 brain teaser:** Why would Mercury be "glowing with happiness" because he knows that his great-grandmother shines "brighter" for him than any other planet?

~ Chapter 16 ~

EXTRAORDINARY ENVIRONMENTS

STILL sitting at the end of Erica's bed and holding an icepack against a very sore spot on his head, Erica's uncle began to read the next chapter of the SOS Transcripts to his niece.

"Chapter Three of the SOS Transcripts . . . *EXTRAORDINARY ENVIRONMENTS*," said Uncle Garwin.

Ø...Ø...Ø...

"An *ENVIRONMENT* is everything that is around you," said Grandfather Neptune.

"Do you mean we all have environments, too?" asked Venus hopefully.

"Well, *SHIMMERING STARS*, Venus . . . of course we do! Your Aphrodite Terra Highlands, your volcanic mountains, your orange sky, and your beautiful, yellow clouds are all part of your environment!" replied Grandfather Neptune.

"Are my polar icecaps part of my environment?" asked Mars.

"Yes, they are. Your wind storms, your rusty soil, your volcanic mountain—Olympus Mons, and your canyon system—Valles Marineris are all part of your environment, too."

"What about me?" pestered Mercury. "What's in my environment?"

"*Everything* you have is part of your environment. Your Caloris Basin, your rocks, your craters, and your steep cliffs are *all* part of your environment," explained Grandfather Neptune.

"Wouldn't humans like my cliffs?" asked Mercury sadly.

"I am sure the humans would love them. They'd think your cliffs are REALLY SHARP," chuckled Grandfather Neptune.

"THEN WHY CAN'T I HAVE HUMANS?" yelled Mercury impatiently.

"Because humans need more than cliffs to stay alive," replied Grandfather Neptune.

"What else do they need, Grandpa? I really want to know because I want humans too!"

"Hmm . . . my memory's not too clear on that. Why don't you explain it to them, Gram."

127

"Well, I know the humans need to live in an environment that does not get too HOT," said Grandmother Uranus.

"Now . . . Mercury, my little dear, your orbit can get as close as 47 million kilometers away from Great-Grandmother Sun, AND your days last much longer than the days on Earth. This gives your great-grandmother the opportunity to raise the temperature in your environment so that it gets at least as high as 400 degrees Celsius," continued Grandmother Uranus. "That sizzling temperature is way too hot for humans . . . so you would have to be farther away from Great-Grandmother Sun if you wanted humans to survive in your environment."

"Oh, I wouldn't like that! I love being so close to my great-grandmother!" sighed Mercury with extreme disappointment.

"I'm sorry you don't have the right kind of environment for humans, but look on the *bright side.*"

"What's that?"

"You can see your great-grandmother more BRIGHTLY than anyone else in our family," replied Grandmother Uranus comfortingly.

"I can?"

"Yes, if you were as far away from her as Earth is, your great-grandmother could appear to be as much as three times smaller."

"Hey, I'm really lucky!" exclaimed Mercury.

Ø ... Ø ... Ø ...

"And *that's* the end of Chapter Three. . . . It is truly amazing, isn't it?"

"It's definitely ASTRONOMICAL!" replied Erica. "I love listening to it, and I'm learning things about the planets that I never knew before. Is it really true that the temperature in Mercury's environment gets higher than 400 degrees Celsius?"

"Yes, it is true, but it also gets really cold there too!" stated Uncle Garwin.

"It does? How could it get so cold if Mercury is that close to the sun?"

"This happens because there is only a sunrise on Mercury every 176 'Earth-days.' As a result of this, the day side of Mercury has a chance to get really hot, and the night side has a chance to get down to -170 degrees Celsius," explained Uncle Garwin.

"That's a *long* day . . . so if you multiply 176 times 24, you would know how many hours there are in one day on Mercury?" asked Erica.

"That is absolutely correct!"

Erica sluggishly stretched her arms above her head and let out a deep yawn.

"Well, how ever many hours that is, it would be too long for me!" she sighed drowsily.

"Okay, Pumpkin, it *is* getting late—and I must say, this '*Earth*-day' has been a *long* day for you."

"A very *exciting* day, too! . . . I never thought my time in the hospital could be so much fun!"

"We definitely will have some more fun tomorrow too, but for now you need to get some sleep," insisted Uncle Garwin.

"Okay, but can I ask you a question?"

"Fire away!"

"I really miss *Moon.* Do you think he is doing okay without me?" asked Erica.

"From what I have been told, *everyone* is making a tremendous fuss over him . . . so I am sure he is doing just fine. Now you get some sleep and don't worry about *anything.* I will see you tomorrow morning, and then I can read the next chapter from the SOS Transcripts to you."

★ **Chapter 17 brain teaser:** If Erica heard seven voices on the Cosmic Communicator, and six of them were planets, who was the other voice?

~ Chapter 17 ~

VOICES IN THE DARK

AFTER Uncle Garwin left, Erica was quite tired, but she was having a difficult time trying to fall asleep. She thought about Moon lying by her empty bed, waiting for her to come home. Erica really did believe that Valen and Mark were taking good care of him, but as she thought about how loyal Moon is, Erica missed him even more.

While holding and petting New Moon, Erica tried to remember what *Moon's* real fur felt like; she knew his fur felt different than New Moon's artificial fur, even though both were smooth and soft. Erica missed petting the top of Moon's head and then sliding her hand down his back all the way to the tip of his tail. She missed his bark, too, and wondered if his bark would sound louder now that her other senses were getting stronger. Furthermore, would she know if Moon was in her room just from his dog smell?

Erica made an effort to pretend that she was home in her own bed with Moon lying on the floor beside her. She was finally getting quite drowsy and starting to fall asleep, but in her deepest memory she remembered lying in bed with her eyes closed, hearing Moon breathe.

He even snores, she thought, which made her laugh but also made her wish Moon was right there with her.

Erica tossed from side to side as she tried to get comfortable and cast away her thoughts about Moon. She began to think about the SOS Transcripts and how she could hardly wait to hear the next chapter in the morning. She reached over onto the bed table to get a drink of water. Erica had learned to be cautious when she did this, so she gradually slid her fingers across the table until they came across an unfamiliar object.

. . . Where is the water, anyway? . . . And what's this thing? she wondered.

Erica carefully picked up the object with both hands and realized it was the Cosmic Communicator.

VOICES IN THE DARK

"*Hey*, I forgot all about this thing," she whispered to herself. Then, she tried to remember the mnemonic device her uncle had taught her.

... *Is it RED PUPPIES SMELL?* ... *No, there were five words;* ... *think, Erica, think,* she told herself.

As she spread her fingers across the four knobs on top and placed her thumb on the bottom knob, Erica remembered the knob on the bottom was *talk*, which meant she could *talk* to Uncle Garwin or someone in her family.

... *Let's see,* she thought. ... ***T*** *is for* ***Talk*** *and* ***T*** *is for* ***Trouble****.* ... *And, I know there's a knob for* "*Listen.*" *So* ... ***L*** *is for* ***Listen****, and* ***L*** *is for* ***Little****.* ... *Then there is* ***P*** *for* ***Puppies*** ... *THAT'S IT!* ... "*LITTLE RED PUPPIES SMELL TROUBLE!*" she yelled loudly.

Erica quickly pushed the first knob ... there they were.

... *VOICES IN THE DARK* ...

rumbling through her Cosmic Communicator as if they were right there in the hospital room all around her. She was instantly transformed; no longer the trapped caterpillar in darkness, she took flight in her mind like the joyful butterfly escaping its cocoon. She listened in total awe and dared to pretend that she was actually spinning right there in space with the planets ... as if she were in the kind of dream that you want to last all night long. However, the voices were *not* a dream, they were *real* . . . coming from space . . . millions of kilometers away . . . directly to *her!*

Even though Erica was blind, listening to the planets' voices through the Cosmic Communicator was more thrilling than anything she had ever experienced in her entire life. She relished every voice, every word, listening to the planets over and over again until she became so familiar with the dialogue she began to recognize what the planets were going to say before they said it.

However, time passed quickly, and soon it was several hours after Erica's bedtime. She was becoming exceptionally tired, but curiosity was stirring in her mind.

. . . *Are the planets really that much like my family, or is it just my imagination?* she thought sleepily. *And is it my imagination that I think about MYSELF when I think about EARTH? . . . Hey, maybe Earth is crying because she's afraid of losing her MOON too! . . . This is BIZZARO! . . . I must be getting delirious or something. . . . But, if I could just listen to the next chapter of the SOS Transcripts—right now. . .*

Unfortunately, Erica knew she had to wait until tomorrow before she could do that.

. . . *I am glad I don't live on Mercury,* she thought hazily. . . . *Then I would have to wait a lot longer before I got a chance to listen to the next chapter. I'd have to wait . . . hmm . . . I think it is one hundred and something . . . 176 times longer. . . . Yeah, that's it! A day lasts 176 times longer on*

Mercury. . . . I wonder how many hours that really would be?

. . . Let's see, thought Erica as she groggily pondered her method of calculation. . . . *176 days times 24 hours . . . that means I have to multiply. . . . First, I multiply 4 times 6, which equals 24. Then, I leave the 4 and carry the 2 over the 7. Next, 4 times 7 equals 28 . . . so, 28 plus . . . hey . . . what number did I carry? . . . I forget! . . . Now I have to start over!*

She tried again . . . and again, but the numbers in Erica's mind were helium balloons that were floating away faster than she could grab onto them.

"This is too hard! I don't think I can do this. I need to *see* the numbers," she grumbled irritably.

Erica was exhausted and exasperated. She lay back down and tried to go to sleep as she pondered the possibility of listening to the recorded voices of the planets once more, thinking it might help her fall asleep this time.

As she picked up the Cosmic Communicator, Erica suddenly remembered that her uncle had given her a blank disc. Carefully spreading her hands across the bed table, she gently searched with her fingers until she found the other disc. Then Erica tediously removed the recorded disc of the planets' voices, slowly placed it on the bed table, and put the blank disc into the Cosmic Communicator. Finally, she pushed the *record* button.

"Entry one—Tuesday night. I'm going to figure out how many hours there are in a day on Mercury," she said confidently. "Okay . . . 176 'Earth-days' times 24 hours . . . I'll start with 4 times 176. . . . 4 times 6 equals 24 . . . then I put down the 4 and carry the 2 over the 7. Now, 4 times 7 equals 28, so I put down the 8 and—wait . . . what number did I carry?"

. . . *Stop asking yourself questions,* she thought mockingly. . . . *Hey, wait a minute . . . I am talking to myself and I can ANSWER myself too! I can listen to what I just said and tell myself what number I just carried!* she realized.

Erica immediately proceeded to listen to herself tell herself that she had carried 2 over 7, and then she marveled at her new discovery.

"This is so awesome . . . it's really working! I can *listen* to myself *tell* myself what I'm thinking!" she whispered excitedly.

By the time Erica found the answer to 176 times 4, she was definitely sure she had found a way to figure out the whole problem and decided to finish it in the morning.

Erica spoke confidently into the Cosmic Communicator, "End of entry one . . . 176 times 4 equals 704 . . . will finish problem tomorrow morning. This is Erica Terrano . . . over and out."

⭐ **Chapter 18 brain teaser:** What name does a "cosmic" person call something that tastes delicious?

~ Chapter 18 ~

THE BRAVE
MISSION

AS SOON as Erica woke up, she reached for the Cosmic Communicator. She listened to her first entry from Tuesday night, and then she continued to record her "day on Mercury" task.

"Second entry—Wednesday morning . . . continue 'day on Mercury' task. . . . I am trying to multiply 24 times 176. . . . I already know that 4 times 176 equals 704. Next, I have to multiply 20 times 176 . . . and then add the product to 704."

Erica continued what she did the night before, *record* and *listen* . . . *record* and *listen* . . . until she got the answer.

"The sum of 704 and 3,520 is 4,224," continued Erica confidently, ". . . so a day on Mercury is 4,224 hours! . . . This is Erica Terrano—over and out!"

"I GOT IT! I GOT IT!" she shouted triumphantly.

Exceptionally thrilled with her accomplishment, Erica could barely wait to tell her uncle. Then, much to her delight, she heard footsteps and was sure they belonged to her uncle.

"Is it 4,224 hours? Uncle Garwin, does a day last 4,224 hours on Mercury?" she asked excitedly.

"What did you say? . . . Your uncle isn't here," said a strange voice. "My name is Steve. I'm a lab technician, and I am here to take you down to the lab for a special blood test."

Like gloomy storm clouds darkening a beautiful, sunny day, Erica's fear maliciously demolished her joy.

"A BLOOD TEST! DO I REALLY HAVE TO?" she yelled nervously.

"It won't take long, Erica," promised Steve as he helped her into the wheel chair.

While she was riding down the hall in the wheel-chair, Erica's fear rapidly grew stronger, and she kept wishing Uncle Garwin was with her . . . to help her feel brave.

. . . *Hey! The Cosmic Communicator*, she thought hopefully, *I can use it to talk to Uncle Garwin when I am in the blood lab!*

Unfortunately, Erica frantically realized that she had forgotten to take the Cosmic Communicator with her. And as she desperately searched every inch of the wheelchair seat, Erica also remembered that she had forgotten to bring New Moon! There she was, on her way to the blood lab all *alone* . . . no uncle to talk to and no "protector" to hold onto . . . nothing there to give her a sense of security. Panic was swiftly gaining control of her thoughts. She wanted to jump up and run away, but the small bit of reason that remained warned her that she would probably just trip over something and hit her head again.

Then, like the welcome burst of sunlight that suddenly reappears through dark storm clouds, Uncle Garwin's advice pierced through Erica's fear.

. . . *He told me to get rid of the negative stuff and think positive thoughts. . . tell myself I am brave and think about things I like. . . . I can do that,* thought Erica. *I am brave . . . I am brave . . . I am brave. . . . I like the planets . . . I want to be an astronaut and go into space someday . . .*

Amazed by the success of her positive thoughts, Erica noticed that her imagination began to take over as quickly as her fear began to fade away. . . . By the time they had reached the elevator, Erica had envisioned herself as an astronaut who was blasting into space on an important mission.

When they got to the lab, Erica was quite relieved that she could not see all of the needles and vials of blood. She closed her eyes and braced herself against the back of her seat as she pretended that her space-craft was breaking through Earth's gravity. Then, as she noticed the obtrusive alcohol smell, she told herself it was just the smell inside of her *new* astronaut helmet. Finally, when she actually felt a little pinch on her arm from the blood test, she imagined it was the security system in her space suit holding her arm in place while she conducted an important experiment in space. . . . After all, an astronaut attempting such an important space mission is surely brave enough to endure a little poke in the arm.

Before she knew it, Erica was back in her room and Uncle Garwin was waiting for her.

"So you were off making discoveries without me, huh?" he asked jokingly.

"No I wasn't!" replied Erica. "Well, *yes* I was! I am a *brave* astronaut and I was off in space on a very special mission!"

Uncle Garwin laughed.

"And they told me you were at the *blood lab!*" he said.

"I really was at the blood lab. I was *afraid* to go, but I pretended that everything happening in the lab was really an exciting adventure in space. I told myself I was a brave astronaut, and then I wasn't afraid anymore."

"Good for you! Using your imagination to over-come fear was a very smart thing to do. . . . Here, I brought you some chocolate chip cookies, so let's celebrate the victory of your *special mission!*"

"Yum, these are so good. They taste like Nana's cookies," said Erica.

"You are absolutely right," replied Uncle Garwin. "Your grandmother *did* bake these cookies."

"I thought so. Chocolate chip cookies from the store feel like a circle, but Nana's cookies are always different shapes. Plus, they are chewy in the middle, crunchy on the edges, and really HUGE," said Erica as she reached into the bag for another cookie.

"I am quite impressed with your observations about chocolate chip cookies. You most certainly seem to be improving the use of your other senses now that your sight is on vacation for awhile."

"Thanks for bringing me *cosmolicious* food to practice with. . . . Oh, by the way, I just remembered something. I practiced using my Cosmic Communicator, too. I made two entries, and I figured out how many hours there are in a day on Mercury."

"You did? Can I listen to it?"

"Sure . . . here," said Erica happily, and then she handed the Cosmic Communicator to her uncle.

Uncle Garwin listened to Erica's recording with admiration, and he felt quite proud of her.

"FANTASTIC JOB, ERICA! It is quite obvious that your head injury has not affected that curious mind you have. You were determined to find the answer, and you did. I am certainly looking forward to working with you as my science partner!" he said.

"I'm excited to be *your* science partner too! Did you bring the rest of the SOS Transcripts?"

"Yes, indeed, I did!"

"What is it called?"

"I named it *A Question of Atmosphere*."

"I can't wait! Does Grandmother Uranus tell Venus and Mars if their environments can have humans?" asked Erica curiously.

"Yes, and there is quite a bit of information in this chapter, so get comfortable."

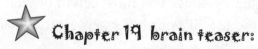 Chapter 19 brain teaser:

Why does the soil on Mars need more practice?

~ Chapter 19 ~

A QUESTION
OF
ATMOSPHERE

UNCLE Garwin settled into the big chair and took a folder out of his briefcase.

"ON WITH THE SOS PROJECT!" he said with a commanding voice, as if he were a captain on a clipper ship that was about to sail across the ocean. Then he began reading the fourth chapter of the SOS Transcripts to Erica.

"Chapter Four . . . A Question of Atmosphere," he stated.

Ø . . . Ø . . . Ø . . .

"How far away is Earth's orbit from Great-Grandmother Sun?" asked Mars.

"Well, I know THAT answer . . . hmm, lets see now," said Grandfather Neptune. "Saturn's moons times Earth's radius . . . that's about 385,000 kilometers . . . "

"Now, dear, I believe 385,000 kilometers is the distance from Earth to Luna," said Grandmother Uranus. "If I remember correctly, Earth's orbit is about 150,000,000 kilometers away from Great-Grandmother Sun."

"*MAGNIFICENT MOONS!* That makes more sense! It is a lot farther from Earth to 'Great-Granny Sun' than it is from Earth to 'Luna Moona,' " chuckled Grandfather Neptune.

"Well, my orbit is farther than 150,000,000 kilometers, I am 240,000,000 kilometers away from our great-grandmother. I wouldn't be too hot for humans, would I?" asked Mars hopefully.

"No, you wouldn't be too hot, but how far away you are from Great-Grandmother Sun is only part of it. You also need an ATMOSPHERE in your environment that can help keep the temperature from getting too hot or too cold. This kind of atmosphere needs to have exactly the right combination of OXYGEN, NITROGEN, and CARBON DIOXIDE. There are very tiny amounts of other gases in Earth's atmosphere, too," explained Grandmother Uranus. "

"Gram, do you think I have the right kind of ATMOSPHERE?" asked Mars.

"Well, your atmosphere is very thin, so it does not retain enough heat from Great-Grandmother Sun. Even on your warmest days the temperature is below zero degrees Celsius. Your WINDSTORMS would be a problem for humans too. They turn your sky a wonderful dark pink, but that is because your rusty soil is blowing through your atmosphere at speeds of over 100 kilometers an hour."

"So, I guess I don't have the right atmosphere for humans either," sighed Mars.

"No, I'm afraid you don't."

Grandmother Uranus's answer was of great concern to Venus. Knowing that her orbit is the closest to Earth's orbit, Venus had not asked her grandmother if she was too close or too far away from Great-Grandmother Sun. She wanted to believe there was still a chance that she could take care of Earth's humans. However, now her grandmother was talking about the right kind of ATMOSPHERE, and Venus had no idea if she had the right atmosphere for humans.

VOICES IN THE DARK

With hope rising from the very depth of her core, Venus asked the question whose answer might crush her hope of taking care of Earth's humans.

"Does my environment have the right kind of ATMOSPHERE for humans?"

"No, love, I am sorry to say that your atmosphere has 97 percent CARBON DIOXIDE, and that is definitely too much carbon dioxide for humans," answered Grandmother Uranus regretfully. "Your yellow clouds and orange sky are amazingly beautiful, but there is too much carbon dioxide in your atmosphere for humans."

Although she felt disappointment ripple throughout every part of her celestial body, Venus continued to show interest in Earth's environment. . . . Even if she could not take care of Earth's humans, maybe she could find another way to help.

"How much carbon dioxide does Earth's atmosphere have?" she asked.

"Earth's atmosphere has less than 1 percent CARBON DIOXIDE."

"WOW!" shouted Mars. "That's a GIGANTIC difference! What about the other gases?"

"Grandpa, do you remember how much OXYGEN Earth's atmosphere has?" asked Grandmother Uranus.

"Hmm . . . uh . . . isn't it a little less than the number of moons YOU have?" answered Grandfather Neptune.

"My dear, you are right! Earth's atmosphere is about 21 percent OXYGEN. And I do remember that there is quite a lot of nitrogen in Earth's atmosphere . . . about 78 percent," replied Grandmother Uranus.

"That makes sense, Grams," agreed Grandfather Neptune. I think there is about 78 percent NITROGEN in Earth's atmosphere because I remember it is about the same as the number of moons Jupiter and I have altogether."

"Earth's atmosphere seems complicated, but I guess that's the reason Earth's environment is so SPECIAL—because she has a special, complicated ATMOSPHERE to keep her from getting too hot or too cold." said Mars.

"Earth's atmosphere also does something else that's very important," said Grandmother Uranus.

"WHAT'S THAT?" asked Mercury anxiously.

"The combination of the gases in Earth's atmosphere gives humans the AIR they need to breathe."

"THEY NEED AIR, TOO?" complained Mercury. "No wonder I can't have humans. I get too hot, and I don't have air!"

"Mercury, it sounds like you have too much HOT AIR!" laughed Uncle Pluto. "Now then, moving on with our discussion, I am quite curious about something. Is Earth's atmosphere the only reason she has the right environment for humans?"

"Not at all! . . . 75 percent of Earth's surface is covered with WATER. She has magnificent salt-water oceans—and rivers, lakes, ponds, and streams made of fresh water. The remaining 25 percent of Earth's surface has mountains, hills, valleys, plateaus, prairies, and deserts that spread across her LAND," said Grandmother Uranus.

"This certainly is interesting," said Uncle Pluto, "but are you quite sure humans actually NEED

AIR, LAND, and WATER?"

"Now, THAT is a complicated question to answer," replied Grandmother Uranus.

"*MISCHIEVOUS METEORS!* It sure is!" added Grandfather Neptune. "That's because humans are not the only LIVING THINGS on Earth that need the AIR, LAND and WATER!"

A QUESTION OF ATMOSPHERE

Uncle Pluto and the children were completely astounded.

"THEY'RE NOT?" yelled Mars and Venus.

"Are you quite sure?" asked Uncle Pluto.

"Grandpa is absolutely right!" said Grandmother Uranus. "Earth has a SPECTACULAR ENVIRONMENT that is full of living things!"

"HEY, THAT'S NOT FAIR!" wailed Mercury.

 Chapter 20 brain teasers:

1. Sound is friendly because it travels in . . .

2. Atoms and molecules are important because they make things that really . . .

~ Chapter 20 ~

A "MATTER" OF MOLECULES

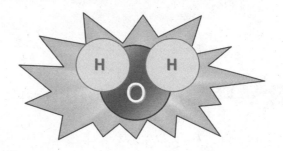

"I MUST say, the more familiar I become with the SOS Transcripts, the more mysterious it all seems to me," stated Uncle Garwin. "I have considered the possibility that since the planets are huge spheres of *matter*, they have enormous numbers of molecules whose movements may be producing sound waves. However, the possibility that the sound waves . . ."

"Wait a minute . . . please slow down, I'm getting confused," interrupted Erica.

"Yes, yes, of course . . . I will certainly try to explain it as simply as I can," replied Uncle Garwin.

"Everything that takes up space and has *mass* is known as *matter*. Air, land, water, plants, animals, humans, this hospital, New Moon, a piece of candy . . . all examples of matter. Now, most "matter" is made of very tiny particles called *atoms*. In fact, atoms are so small you could fit billions of them on the head of a pin. However, even though there are more atoms in a single grain of sand than you could possibly count in a lifetime, there are only about 100 different *types* of atoms that we know of—such as hydrogen, oxygen, iron, copper, carbon . . . and the list goes on.

"Amazingly enough, atoms are made of smaller particles as well. In the center of each atom, there is a *nucleus*, which is made of *protons* and *neutrons*. There are also tiny particles in an atom called *electrons,* which are constantly moving around the outside of the nucleus," continued Uncle Garwin.

"In a way, every atom is similar to a 'mini' *solar system* because the electrons move around the nucleus of the atom just as planets move around the sun. The main difference is that electrons do *not* have a specific orbit to travel in as planets do. . . . In the early 20th century, a Danish scientist named Niels Bohr developed a theory stating that electrons move in *orbits* around the nucleus of the atom. However, since then, scientists have discovered that the electrons move in many *different* directions around the nucleus of the atom rather than traveling in a single, definite orbit.

"Now then, continuing on with atoms. . . . When atoms join together, sometimes they *share* their

VOICES IN THE DARK

electrons. AND, when atoms share electrons, *molecules* are formed," explained Uncle Garwin. "For example, when two atoms of hydrogen share electrons with one atom of oxygen, a *water molecule* is formed—which is commonly represented by the formula H_2O. In this formula, 'H_2' represents two atoms of hydrogen and 'O' represents one atom of oxygen. Therefore, different combinations of atoms create different types of molecules, which are represented by different formulas."

Erica limply tipped her head onto New Moon and let out a big sigh.

. . . Oh, no, she thought. *I HAD to go and tell him I was confused! Well . . . I guess if I am going to be his science partner for the SOS Project, I should pay attention to information that he thinks is important.*

Taking a cue from Erica's sigh, Uncle Garwin attempted to *finish* his explanation.

"It comes down to this," he said. "Matter is made of atoms. When atoms share their electrons, molecules are formed. *Sound* is created when molecules *bump* into other molecules and make sound waves. Now, since the planets are very large and contain a lot of matter, there could be a lot of sound waves coming from them."

"I get *that* part . . . when molecules bump into each other, they can make sound waves—and there is a lot of matter on the planets, so there could be a lot of sound, too," said Erica with a proud grin.

152

A "MATTER" OF MOLECULES

"Yes, you've got it," answered Uncle Garwin, "but HERE is where the *mystery* begins. . . . We do not even know if the planets have any form of intelligence. Furthermore, even if the planets actually do have intelligence, how are their intelligent thoughts becoming the sounds of their voices . . . voices that speak our language?

"When humans speak, the movement of molecules in their vocal cords helps create sound waves," continued Uncle Garwin, "but I find it extremely unlikely that the planets have vocal cords! And even if the planets actually have intelligent thoughts and are able to speak our language, then how are their conversations traveling through space? . . . Scientists believe that sound cannot travel through space at all, so conversations between the . . ."

"WHAT! SOUND CAN'T TRAVEL THROUGH SPACE?" yelled Erica disappointedly.

"Calm down, partner . . . this is all part of the mystery we need to solve. You see, we hear sounds here on Earth because Earth's *air* is a form of matter. When the molecules of Earth's air bump into each other they can make sound waves. And sound travels very quickly through the air on Earth . . . about 344 meters per second.

"However, there is no *air* in space. In fact, scientists classify space as a *vacuum*. Now, a *true* vacuum contains no atoms . . . no molecules. . . . no matter at all; therefore, sound cannot travel in a *true* vacuum. Nevertheless, aside from the planets, stars and other large celestial bodies, there are *tiny* particles of matter out there within the darkness of space—which means space itself is not actually a *true* vacuum. So, the possibility exists that sound can travel through space, but I do not think the planets' voices are actually traveling through space in the form of sound waves," stated Uncle Garwin.

"But how can you know that for sure?" asked Erica.

"Well, the tiny particles of matter in space are very far away from each other, so it would take a long time for any molecules out there to bump into each other. Therefore, if the planets' voices are traveling through space in the form of sound waves, it would certainly take much longer than our lifetime for their voices to reach each other and then reach the SOS Receiver."

"Then why did you make a 'SOUNDS OF SPACE' RECEIVER if it's practically *impossible* for sound to travel through space?" inquired Erica curiously.

"Well now, I guess I should have expected *that* question," admitted Uncle Garwin. "You see, the SOS Receiver is purely an experimental type of technology, and I realize now that the name I gave it is somewhat misleading. When I constructed it, I was interested in detecting unusual *emanations* from space, rather than actual sound waves. However, when I gave it to you as a gift, the 'Sounds Of Space Receiver' seemed like a better name than the 'Unusual Space Emanation Detector.'

"Nonetheless, I didn't expect planets' voices to come rumbling through the SOS Receiver, and now I feel like I have confused you. Even though the possibility exists that the planets' voices themselves may be the result of sound waves, I'M SURE THE PLANETS' VOICES ARE NOT TRAVELING THROUGH SPACE IN THE FORM OF SOUND WAVES," stated Uncle Garwin rather loudly, as though he wanted to convince himself as well as Erica. "Their voices must be traveling through an . . . an unknown phenomenon—something that is yet to be discovered," he added hesitantly.

"BIZZARO! I guess you really did receive unusual *em . . . a . . . nations* with the SOS Receiver! This is so exciting! Just think how amazed everyone will be if we figure out what this UNKNOWN PHENOMENON is!" exclaimed Erica.

"You mean WHEN we figure it out!" stated Uncle Garwin confidently. "In the meantime, we must continue to consider even the smallest detail from the SOS Transcripts as an important clue—and keep your wonderful, creative imagination flowing. . . . We are definitely in the midst of quite a *special* mission, and the answer to this mystery may be more phenomenal than we realize!"

⭐ **Chapter 21 brain teaser:** What kind of breakfast food would you be if you were on Venus?

~ Chapter 21 ~

THE GREENHOUSE EFFECT

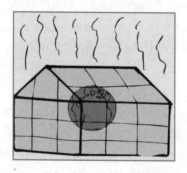

"I **HAVE** been trying very hard to pay close attention to details in the SOS Transcripts," said Erica, "and I've also learned some new things about Earth's environment. I never knew that Earth's atmosphere was a *part* of her environment. . . . I thought that Earth's environment was just the things you can see or touch, like grass, trees, water in the ocean—stuff like that. Now I know that Earth's atmosphere gives us air, and the atmosphere and air are part of Earth's environment."

"Do you remember what Grandmother Uranus said about the gases in Earth's air?" asked Uncle Garwin.

"I remember Earth has about 21 percent oxygen, because 21 is a little less than the number of moons Grandmother Uranus has," replied Erica. "Plus, Earth also has about 78 percent nitrogen. I remember that because 78 is close to the number of moons Grandfather Neptune and Jupiter have altogether."

"That's correct! You certainly have been paying close attention to the details! Earth's atmosphere consists of about 21 percent oxygen and about 78 percent nitrogen, along with carbon dioxide and tiny amounts of other gases."

"I was wondering about those other gases . . . what kinds of gases are they?"

"There's argon, neon, helium, methane, hydrogen and even krypton," answered Uncle Garwin.

"SUPERMANNNN!" Erica burst out laughing. "Do we really have KRYPTON on Earth? Isn't that *dangerous* stuff?"

"Green 'make-believe' kryptonite is dangerous to *Superman*, but 'Mother Nature' seems to have *real* krypton gas under control for us humans! However, *carbon dioxide* is a type of gas we need to be concerned about."

"Why do we have to be concerned about carbon dioxide?"

"Too much carbon dioxide causes something called the *greenhouse effect,*" stated Uncle Garwin.

"You mean mom's greenhouse has too much carbon dioxide?"

"*NO*, but the point is . . . it can get really *hot* inside of a greenhouse."

"I know it gets too hot in there for me! Mom always has to keep the windows open when the sun shines. She says if she doesn't, then it will get too hot in there for the plants, too," said Erica.

"That's exactly what happens when there is too much carbon dioxide in an atmosphere; it gets too hot!"

"Hey, what is carbon dioxide anyway?"

"Good question, indeed," replied Uncle Garwin. Carbon dioxide is a gas molecule that is made of one atom of carbon and two atoms of oxygen, so the formula is CO_2. Most importantly, carbon dioxide happens to be a molecule that absorbs heat. Therefore, when there is too much carbon dioxide in the atmosphere, too much heat gets absorbed in the atmosphere. . . . Then the temperature becomes too hot for living things in the environment.

"Furthermore, we can't open windows to let the heat and carbon dioxide out of an atmosphere. The atmosphere on Venus has 97 percent carbon dioxide, so her temperature can get hotter than the temperature on Mercury, even though she is farther away from the sun."

"I always thought it would be exciting to be an astronaut and go to Venus, but if mom's greenhouse gets too hot for me, I know I wouldn't like the temperature on Venus," said Erica.

"I'm sure you're right about that. I don't think anybody would like the *atmospheric pressure* on Venus either," said Uncle Garwin.

"You mean her *gravity?*"

"Not quite. Gravity is a force that pulls molecules toward each other. On the other hand, atmospheric pressure comes from the *weight* of molecules, and carbon dioxide molecules are much heavier than the air molecules on Earth. The atmospheric pressure on Venus is about 90 times greater than the atmospheric pressure on Earth. . . . It's like being about 3,000 feet under the ocean—it would smash you as flat as a pancake," explained Uncle Garwin.

"Yikes! I wouldn't like the *pressure* on Venus either . . . but what about her *gravity?* Does she have gravity? Is it 90 times stronger that Earth's gravity?" asked Erica curiously.

"You might think so. However, Venus actually has a little less gravity than Earth. . . . Do you happen to know how much you weigh?"

"Oh, about 85 pounds."

"Then you'd only weigh about 76 pounds on Venus," stated Uncle Garwin.

"Until I got smashed as flat as a pancake," laughed Erica. "So, how much would I weigh on Mars?"

"You would only weigh about 31 pounds on Mars; however, you would be able to jump really high!"

"That would be fun, but I wouldn't like being cold all the time. You know, I feel sorry for Venus . . . and Mars, too. They really wanted to help Earth by taking care of her humans, but we'd be hot pancakes on Venus and frozen popsicles on Mars!" joked Erica.

She wrapped her arms around her stomach and laughed.

"Yummm . . . hot pancakes and frozen popsicles . . . I'm making myself hungry!" she said. "I wonder if I would miss being able to eat my favorite foods if I were an astronaut in space. Maybe I would get lonely up there in space, too, because sound can't travel through space so the astronauts . . . hey, wait a minute. . ."

⭐ **Chapter 22 brain teaser:** Why does Erica think her grandfather called her a "smart chicken"?

~ Chapter 22 ~
MOM

MRS. Terrano silently appeared in the doorway. She gently placed a large cloth bag on a small chair by the door and motioned to her brother-in-law.

"Excuse me a minute, Erica. I'll be right back," said Uncle Garwin, and then he walked out into the hallway.

"HEY! I SMELL FOOD!" bellowed Erica . . . her senses were becoming too keen to miss the pungent intrusion.

. . . *It smells spicy*, she thought, *kind of the way burritos smell . . .*

As she sniffed the air more thoroughly, Erica felt like Moon sniffing around in the kitchen when there was food on the counter. She could not see the food, but she knew it was there.

. . . *Or could it be egg rolls?* she wondered.

"UNCLE GARWIN, are you there? Is someone else here? I smell spicy food!"

"It seems we can't sneak *anything* by you anymore," replied Erica's mother.

"MOM!" yelled Erica joyfully. She reached out to hug her mother, and found herself holding on very tightly, not wanting to let go. This sudden, overwhelming joy came as a surprise to Erica. Because she had been so concerned about missing Moon, Erica had not realized just how much she missed her parents too.

"This is quite an affectionate reception," replied Mrs. Terrano as she lovingly returned Erica's lengthy hug.

Erica didn't know what to say. She was feeling a little embarrassed about having such an emotional reaction to her mother's visit. After all, why would an eleven-year old be so happy to see her mother if she just saw her the day before?

. . . *I've been away from my parents lots of times and I never felt like this when I saw them again,* she thought. *Wait! . . . I didn't SEE my mom because I can't SEE anything! . . . Is that why I'm hugging my mom for so long, to tell myself that she is really here?*

"Is it *me* . . . or the smell of food that's making you so happy?" asked Mrs. Terrano.

"It's BOTH!" answered Erica, finally pulling away from her mother. "I miss you, AND it smells like I'm in the food court at the mall, trying to decide what to eat. . . . Is it Mexican food or Asian food?"

"It's BOTH!" laughed Mrs. Terrano. I brought burritos, egg rolls, and fortune cookies. I have some carrot and cucumber slices, too . . . freshly picked this morning by your dad. "

"Thanks, Mom."

"Here you go, Garwin, I brought plenty for you, too. I thought you might be here. I really appreciate the time you've been spending with Erica. I wish I could have gotten here more often myself. I know it's been lonely for her in the hospital."

"Not anymore!' interrupted Erica. "Uncle Garwin gave me a *Cosmic Communicator!*"

"A WHAT?"

"A *COSMIC COMMUNICATOR!*" repeated Erica excitedly, feeling like a bubble ready to burst. She wanted to tell her mom all about the SOS Receiver . . . the talking planets . . . the SOS Transcripts . . . the SOS Project . . . but Erica knew she had to wait.

"It's like a cell phone," continued Erica. "Plus, it's like a tape recorder, but it uses little discs instead of tapes. I even figured out how many hours there are in a day on Mercury!"

"Excellent job, Pumpkin," said Mrs. Terrano affectionately.

"Everybody has been calling me 'Pumpkin' a lot lately. Grandpa even called me his *poultry* . . . uh . . . *poultry-studious* pumpkin. Does that mean I am a *smart chicken*?" asked Erica jokingly.

Bawk! The Square root of 81 is 9.

"It's *PUL-CHRI-TU-DI-NOUS*," laughed Uncle Garwin. "It means *pretty.*"

"Well, anyway, it's been a long time since everyone called me 'Pumpkin.' The last time I remember everyone calling me that name was when I had the *chicken pox* during summer vacation and everyone felt sorry for me. So, is everybody feeling sorry for me again?"

"I don't think it's because we feel sorry for you. I think it's because accidents have a way of reminding us how much we love and appreciate the person who has been hurt. . . . Some of the qualities we appreciate about you the most are your courage, perseverance, and imagination. Maybe everyone has been calling you 'Pumpkin' because it reminds us of these qualities that you have," said Mrs. Terrano as she smiled at Uncle Garwin and started swinging her finger back and forth between him and Erica, hoping he would back up her explanation.

"That makes sense to me," he added with reassurance. I don't think any of the adults in the family will ever forget your 'pumpkin frenzy.' "

"Well, I think it's silly, so don't remind me of it! I can't believe that *Cinderella* was my favorite story!" said Erica in a rather embarrassed way.

"It may seem silly to you, but it's very endearing to us," replied Erica's mother. "Sitting alone in the corner of the garden for two hours with your arms wrapped around a pumpkin, waiting for your fairy godmother to turn it into a carriage and whisk you off to a castle showed a lot of courage, perseverance, and imagination for a four-year old. Especially since it was pitch black out there in the garden. . . . There was a *new moon*, so it was very dark outside, and someone had turned off the back porch light. I admit we were frantic because we couldn't find you, but when we realized what you were trying to do, we were very impressed."

Mrs. Terrano wrapped her arms around Erica and gave her a warm hug.

"And we've been very impressed with you these last few days too. Uncle Garwin even told me about your 'special mission,' " she said lovingly.

Erica's heart sank into her stomach. She felt deceived . . . betrayed . . . her thoughts raged.

. . . How could he?. . . Uncle Garwin said we couldn't tell anyone yet! I WANTED to tell someone too! It was my SOS Receiver! . . . I can't trust anyone! she thought angrily.

Heartbroken and resentful, Erica carelessly shoved New Moon onto the bed table and then plunged her head onto her pillow. But in her haste, Erica knocked over Mrs. Terrano's cup of coffee.

"Oh, I'm sorry! I shouldn't have put my coffee on the bed table. Don't be upset; it's not your fault!" said Mrs. Terrano as she tried to comfort Erica by lightly stroking her dark, shiny hair. "I'm just glad it wasn't hot. I'm going to have to be more careful from now on."

. . . *Bizzaro! This is a switch*, thought Erica. . . . *I'm usually the one who has to apologize because I put things where they don't belong. Now my mom is apologizing to me! . . . She thinks this is her fault! I guess she doesn't even know the real reason I am so upset. . . . Uncle Garwin should know! HE SHOULD KNOW WHAT HE DID!*

Now that she was blind, Erica made it a point to put things back in the same place so she could find them again, and she suddenly remembered that she had left the Cosmic Communicator on the bed table.

"Is the Cosmic Communicator ruined? . . . And, did the coffee spill on New Moon?" she asked angrily.

Erica's inability to see what had happened added fuel to the fire; her thoughts were raging flames blowing in the wind.

. . . *Oh sure,* she thought furiously, *I can't even look for myself to SEE if the coffee spilled on them! I can't do ANYTHING except sit in bed and listen to my uncle tell me fibs, and I bet the SOS Transcripts are nothing but a big joke too!*

MOM

"The Cosmic Communicator is waterproof. It is quite a durable piece of equipment, so I'm sure it's not damaged," said Uncle Garwin. "Nonetheless, I'm not so sure about the disc that was on the table. Which one is it?"

"The one you recorded for me," muttered Erica indifferently. "You know, the one from our 'special mission,' " she added sarcastically.

"Well now, don't worry, that's not a problem at all. I can always record another one," answered Uncle Garwin in a cheerful manner.

"New Moon survived his coffee bath without any major damage . . . I think his fur is waterproof also," added Erica's mother. "Most of the coffee came off onto the towel I just used to dry him with, but I don't think I can say the same for your robe—it definitely needs to be washed. It just so happens that I brought a clean one with me. I'll help you change."

⭐ **Chapter 23 brain teaser:** Why doesn't Erica want to go on her incredible "journey"?

~ Chapter 23 ~

TOMORROW

You are about to
on an incredible

ERICA felt exceptionally foolish and mis-
understood as broody thoughts bubbled in her mind.

. . . *My uncle tricks me and doesn't even say
he's sorry! They're sitting over there jibber-
jabbering like my feelings aren't important at all.*

. . . *Didn't he even bother to tell her that our
special mission was supposed to be just between
him and me? . . . We BOTH said we wouldn't tell
anyone yet!*

As Erica sat there in total silence, she listened to her empty stomach growling inside of her like an angry grizzly bear, and she *felt* as annoyed as a hungry grizzly bear herself. She wanted to growl out loudly, but the delicious scent of the food convinced her to eat now and complain later.

Erica crunched into the egg roll, sliding the crisp greasy flakes between her fingers. Then she squeezed the soft, mushy beans through the tortilla shell until they plopped into her mouth. In her dark world of melancholy, Erica's senses gradually began to amuse and console her.

Smelling the sweetness of the fabric softener on her clean robe and the remnants of the coffee spill on New Moon reminded her of a typical Saturday at home, when the coffee pot perked all morning and the smell of clean laundry permeated the air long after the clothes had been folded and put away. . . . Listening to the familiar sounds of the elevator bell and chattering at the nurses' station outside the door gave her a sense of comfort also, and Erica realized that she had become quite accustomed to her new life in the hospital.

"You're unusually quiet," commented Uncle Garwin lightly.

Erica reluctantly muttered a response. "Yep," she said dryly.

Uncle Garwin and Erica's mom exchanged perplexed glances and shrugged their shoulders.

"You're not still upset about the coffee spill, are you?" asked Mrs. Terrano.

"NO, MOM," snapped Erica. "I'm not upset about the coffee spill!"

"Here, pick a cookie from the bag and I'll read your fortune to you, maybe that will lift your spirits," said Mrs. Terrano, and then she placed a bag filled with fortune cookies on her daughter's lap.

Erica haphazardly shoved her hand around in the bag, just so she could listen to the crinkly wrappers. If she couldn't *look* at the cookies, she at least wanted to *hear* them. Somehow, her choice would seem more legitimate if she made a lot of noise before she picked a fortune cookie.

Finally, Erica pulled a cookie out of the bag. "This one," she mumbled, handing it to her mother.

"It says . . . **You are about to embark on an incredible journey.**"

"Not much of a chance for *that*," Erica retorted.

"Well, here's something that will definitely brighten your spirits. I happen to know a very 'incredible journey' you'll be taking tomorrow," said Mrs. Terrano with a cheerful tone.

"What's that?" replied Erica monotonously.

"I have good news! . . . You can finally go HOME from the hospital!"

"Well, that's fantastic!' exclaimed Uncle Garwin.

Erica was silent. Just a few days ago she wanted to hear those words more than anything else in the world. Now, the news was unexpected and seemed to have lost its importance. Being blind in the hospital suddenly seemed safer to her than being blind at home.

"Honey, did you hear me? You can go HOME tomorrow!"

"Are you sure it's okay? I mean, what if Matthew leaves something on the floor and I trip over it and hit my head again?"

"Everything will be just fine," assured Erica's mother. "Matthew is going to stay with your great-grandmother for a few days. And the doctor wants you to stay in bed for awhile after you get home, so you don't have to worry about tripping over anything."

"Why do I have to stay in bed? Doesn't it mean I'm getting better if I can go home?" asked Erica skeptically.

"You *are* getting better, but your recent blood work revealed some complications developing from your original medication. The doctor started you on a new prescription today, so he just wants you to stay in bed for a couple of days as a precaution. . . . We'll just have to make sure that Moon stays right there with you while you're in bed."

. . . MOON! . . . Moon will be with me! How could I have forgotten about him? Erica asked herself. *. . . Who cares if I have to stay in bed? Moon will be with me!*

Erica's sense of relief and excitement exploded into words like colorful confetti spurting out of a party popper.

"I CAN'T WAIT TO SEE HIM! . . . IS HE OKAY? DOES HE MISS ME?" she shouted excitedly.

TOMORROW

"He is just fine, and he has been getting lots of attention," replied Mrs. Terrano. "In fact, he's at the park with Mark and Valen right now, so I'd better get going. Besides, we don't want to be late for his le . . . uh . . . feeding him his dinner. You know how hungry he gets!"

Mrs. Terrano gave Erica another big hug.

"I love you . . . and I am so happy you're coming home," she said.

Erica hugged back as hard as she could.

"I'm glad too! Give Moon a *humongous* hug for me, and tell him I am coming HOME!"

"I will! I'll see you in the morning," said Mrs. Terrano, and then she grinned at Uncle Garwin and rushed out the door.

⭐ **Chapter 24 brain teaser:** Why was there something "fishy" about Erica's anger?

~ Chapter 24 ~

AN HONEST MISTAKE

AFTER her mother left, Erica found herself facing an uncomfortable dilemma. She wanted to give her uncle a big, angry stare . . . big and angry enough to make him ask her why she was so cross. However, the way her uncle tends to pace back and forth, Erica was not certain *what* she would actually end up staring at. And, if he was pacing, her uncle might not be looking at her anyway. . . . Her other option was to come right out and tell her uncle that she was angry and get it over with as soon as possible, instead of waiting for him to say something to her.

In the end, she resorted to the quickest option. Erica decided that she was too angry to lie around and wait for her uncle to notice her. She was going to speak up and make sure that he did! After all, Erica knew she would look ridiculous directing a big, angry stare toward the door . . . the wall . . . the bathroom sink. At least if she spoke up, he would answer her . . . she would know where he was. Then, she could yell at him *and* give him an angry stare.

"YOU SAID WE COULDN'T TELL ANYONE! WHY DID YOU TELL MOM?" she shouted with the angriest face she could muster.

Uncle Garwin was completely dumbfounded. He quickly moved the small chair by the door across the room and placed it next to Erica's bed. Then, he sat down beside her.

"What do you mean?" he asked.

"YOU TOLD HER ABOUT THE SOS TRANSCRIPTS," growled Erica.

"Whatever gave you that idea?"

"MOM SAID YOU TOLD HER ABOUT OUR SECRET MISSION!" yelled Erica loudly. In fact, her voice was so loud that one of the nurses popped her head in the door to see if everything was okay.

"Is that what you've been so upset about? Now, calm down. The nurse is here checking to see if you're okay," replied Uncle Garwin fretfully.

Erica strained to lower her voice. "I'm O . . . kay! And YES, that's what I'm upset about. You said we weren't supposed to say anything to anybody, but YOU DID!"

"No . . . I didn't tell anyone, Pumpkin."

. . . *URRR* . . . Anger consumed Erica's thoughts like a shark chomping on its prey. . . . *He's lying!* . . . *Plus he's calling me "Pumpkin," like I'm too silly or young to know the difference!*

"WHY are you LYING to me?" asked Erica.

"Uh . . . I'm not lying . . . I am sure this is just a misunderstanding," assured Uncle Garwin.

"What's going on then?" snapped Erica. "What part don't I understand?"

"Your mother meant 'your' mission, not 'our' mission. She was talking about your trip to the blood lab, not our SOS Project," explained Uncle Garwin.

Erica sat completely frozen, but somehow she managed to crack out an apology.

"S-sorry."

"It's okay," replied Uncle Garwin kindly. "It was an *honest* mistake. I would be angry too if I thought someone betrayed my trust and then lied about it. Honesty is very important to me, so you can be sure that I will always tell you the truth. Moreover, I am glad you said something to me; I wouldn't want you to lie there fuming with anger all evening."

Erica was incredibly sorry that she had even doubted her uncle for a second. She knew better. He had always been there for her. He was the one who talked her parents into letting her get a puppy. After the pumpkin incident, he was sure that she would need a smart dog like a German shepherd to stay with her and protect her if she wandered off on her own. Then, after he had given her the puppy, he had read these words to her from a big pumpkin card.

> Take this puppy with you
> whenever you roam . . .
> He will grow into a big dog soon.
> If you get lost, he will take you
> home . . .
> Even if it's dark and there's no
> moon.

That was the reason she had named her new puppy 'Moon.' Erica still keeps the card on her bookshelves and reads it every year on Moon's birthday.

Erica apologized again. "I'm soooo sorry. I really messed up."

"It's okay; everybody makes mistakes. Nobody's perfect, that's for sure. Nonetheless, keep in mind that it is always a good idea to try to learn from your mistakes. Next time, remember, you can count on me to keep my word. So, if you think there's a problem, talk to me about it instead of getting angry and yelling at me before you know what the truth is."

"That's makes sense. I don't like it when I get mad at people I care about . . . like when I got mad at Mark for telling the secret about my accident before I knew the truth about what really happened," replied Erica humbly.

Uncle Garwin raised Erica's hand and gave her a "high five."

"Are we cool?"

Erica took a deep breath and let out a big sigh of relief.

"We're cool!" she said, and then she tried to return the "high five" and ended up slapping her uncle's chin!

"OUCH! Are you sure?" snickered Uncle Garwin.

Erica laughed contentedly . . . all was well again.

⭐ **Chapter 25 brain teaser:** Why should Uncle Garwin have checked his watch when he was explaining ancient wisdom to Erica?

~ Chapter 25 ~

ERICA'S
EMPATHEORY

"*UNCLE* Garwin, there is something I was going to ask you just before Mom came to visit. . . . I remember you said that it's practically impossible for sound to travel through space, but I thought the astronauts can talk to us from space," said Erica.

"The astronauts *can* talk to us from space. However, their voices don't travel to Earth through sound waves. Their voices travel through *electromagnetic radio waves,* because electromagnetic waves definitely *can* travel through space," stated Uncle Garwin.

"Well, maybe the planets' voices are traveling through those electric . . . uh . . ."

"*Electromagnetic* radio waves . . . not likely. Even though we know that electromagnetic radio waves can travel through space, there are other important facts that we need to consider. It can take up to 20 minutes just for a simple message to travel from Mars to Earth through electromagnetic radio waves. Now, just think how far the planets' voices would have to travel to reach each other. . . . We would hear long delays during their conversations if their voices were traveling through electromagnetic radio waves, and we're not hearing any delays at all!" replied Uncle Garwin.

"What about SOLAR STORMS! Didn't Mars say something about SOLAR STORMS? . . . Maybe they have something to do with all of this! Maybe the solar storms are causing the unknown phenomenon! I remember learning that they can cause unusual things to happen!" suggested Erica.

"Well, solar storms could actually *block* the transmission of electromagnetic radio waves," explained Uncle Garwin.

"Hey . . . Mars said the solar storms would keep Earth from hearing what they were saying. So, if the solar storms are blocking the planet's voices from getting to Earth, wouldn't that mean the planets' voices are traveling through electro . . . magnetic radio waves?" insisted Erica.

"That would seem to indicate a connection between the planets' voices and electromagnetic radio waves. However, as I stated previously, we would hear long delays if the planets' voices were traveling through electromagnetic radio waves. So, I am inclined to believe that the mysterious phenomenon which is transporting the planets' voices might actually be coming from a dimension of time and space that scientists on our planet have not yet discovered!" replied Uncle Garwin.

"Then, maybe ALIENS are doing this! Maybe ALIENS know about another dimension of time and space, and they are making the planets voices come through the SOS Receiver! . . . Do you think it could really be ALIENS?" asked Erica excitedly.

"Well now, Erica, I should know better than to underestimate your imagination. Although, I suppose we can't rule out the possibility that it might be aliens. I'll contact Professor Gazer about that. She has a private research center in Scotland where they monitor space for signs of intelligent life. Maybe she is aware of some unusual signals from space," suggested Uncle Garwin. "I'll make a note of that right now, so I won't forget."

As Erica's uncle opened his briefcase to get his notepad, he saw the large manila envelope that had arrived in the mail before he came to the hospital that day.

"Speaking of Professor Gazer, this package was delivered to my house with your name on it," said Uncle Garwin, gently placing the envelope in Erica's hands.

She quickly unwrapped the package. Inside there was a card and a rectangular, velvet box. Erica had been taught to always read the card before she opened a present. But, since Erica could not *see* the card, she immediately opened the box. It contained an unusual necklace with many spherical stones of various sizes . . . nine altogether.

Uncle Garwin gently placed the necklace around Erica's neck, and then he opened the card.

"This card has a beautifully colored picture of the solar system on it, and there is a message inside," he said. "I'll read it to you."

Dear Erica,

Your uncle told me about your unfortunate accident, and I send best wishes for a speedy recovery. If there is anything I can do, I've already informed your uncle that I am more than willing to help. We are in the process of repairing damages from the fire at the observatory and hope to be using it soon.

This necklace is a reminder that you have an open invitation to visit the observatory at any time. It represents the planets in our solar system. The largest stone is Jupiter, and the stones are arranged according to their distances from the sun.

Sincerely,
Professor Gazer

"Professor Gazer must be a really nice lady. I never even met her and she wants to help me. Plus, she sent me this awesome gift."

"She is a very compassionate person, and this *is* an incredible gift," replied Uncle Garwin, admiring the necklace. "The stones are really beautiful."

"Are the stones different colors?" asked Erica.

"Yes, they're very similar to the colors of the planets."

Erica quickly found Jupiter and placed her index finger and thumb around the stone to the right.

"Is Mars a rusty red color?" she asked.

"Yes, it is."

"Erica touched the stone to the right of Mars.

"Is Earth blue and white?"

"Right again. Earth appears to be a blue star sapphire," answered Uncle Garwin.

"What about this next one, is it yellow and orange?"

"Yes, the Venus stone is a deep orange-yellow. It actually looks quite a bit like a golden topaz."

"And the Mercury stone, what does it look like?"

"It's different shades of gray."

"I really love this necklace!" said Erica as she slid her fingers from Mercury around her neck to Pluto. "Hey, wait a minute . . . there's no SUN!"

"Maybe the person who *wears* it is supposed to be the sun. Indeed, that is a superb reminder for you to keep a positive attitude," commented Uncle Garwin.

"After the way I acted today, I probably do need another reminder."

"Actually, it seems to me that you are beginning to understand the ancient wisdom of 'TIME.' "

"The ancient wisdom of *time*? What is *that*?" asked Erica.

"It says that for everything there is a season . . . such as a time to weep and a time to laugh; a time to lose and a time to get; a time to keep silent and a time to speak. Therefore, it is important not to give up hope when times seem hard, because better times will come again."

"I guess I *am* beginning to figure that out. This must be my 'time' to be blind . . . oh, and *brave*, too."

"Blind, brave, and quite a bit wiser . . . I'm very proud of you," said Uncle Garwin affectionately. "I must say, your attitude has definitely changed since I walked in here on Monday. . . .You were so sad and frightened. You thought that losing your sight was the most terrible thing in the world, and all of your thoughts centered around everything that you didn't like about being blind."

"And now I like to think about the SOS Project. It makes me feel good to know that I can help you even though I am blind," replied Erica happily.

"Indeed, this SOS Project certainly is the biggest mystery I've ever attempted to unravel, and I am glad that I have your help! This is truly quite a phenomenon. . . . The planets talking . . . their voices mysteriously coming through the SOS Receiver . . . AND, my computer printing their conversations in the form of a story. . . .

"I also must say that I am quite intrigued with the strong similarity between the planets and our family. When I made up the story about the Cosmic Family, I *never* in my *wildest* imagination would have conceived that it could possibly be anything more than a science fairytale!" stated Uncle Garwin quite firmly.

"So the similarities are definitely *not* our imagination? . . . I KNEW IT!" Erica yelled decisively. "Earth and the solar children . . . Uncle Pluto . . . Grandfather Neptune and Grandmother Uranus . . . they all remind me of our family. This SOS Project is getting so exciting, and I think it's going to be totally awesome to be your partner! What do you want me to do?"

"I brought you a disc that has *A Question of Atmosphere* on it. I want you to listen to the disc several times," said Uncle Garwin.

"I can't *wait* to do *that!*"

"That's the kind of enthusiasm I like to hear! Now, pay close attention to the similarities between the planets and our family; maybe it will offer some clues about *why* EARTH IS CRYING. Remember, Erica, we must investigate this mystery from all aspects. Not only do we need to discover HOW this is happening, we need to find out WHY this is happening!"

"I have already thought about the similarities a lot, and I think I *might* understand why Earth is crying," replied Erica proudly. "I think maybe Earth is crying for the same reason that I was crying after my accident."

"Hmm . . . very interesting . . . it seems you are basing your theory on *EMPATHY*," replied Uncle Garwin.

"I'm basing it on WHAT?" asked Erica with a confused look on her face.

"*Empathy*. It means you understand how someone feels because you have had a similar experience yourself. However, I'm quite curious. What do *you* and Earth have in common that makes you think you know why she's crying?" asked Uncle Garwin.

"One reason is because we both have a younger brother who's a pest . . . a younger sister who likes to be helpful . . . an older brother who's responsible . . . a funny grandpa . . . a really sweet grandma, AND a *far-out* uncle. BUT that's not why I think she's crying. That just made me start to think about how much our families are the same. All the stuff about Earth's "secret' got me thinking about why Earth might be crying," answered Erica confidently.

"You see, Earth is crying about a big secret that she doesn't want anyone to know about, and I was crying about a big secret that I didn't want anyone to know about—you know, the secret about my accident. Plus, Earth's secret went from her older brother to her sister . . . to her younger brother . . . to her uncle . . . and then to her grandparents, just like my secret did."

"I must say, that is very observant of you. I surely didn't notice that particular similarity. Have you noticed anything else?"

"Yep, my secret was that Moon accidentally knocked me over, and I didn't want Moon to get blamed for it because I was afraid my parents wouldn't let me keep him for a pet anymore. Then when I went blind, I was afraid of the darkness. So, it could be something like that for Earth too—and I thought of a theory. Would you like to hear it?" asked Erica eagerly.

"Certainly, this is quite interesting; please go on," said Uncle Garwin.

"Okay . . . maybe some accident happened to Earth and part of her environment isn't working the way it should, so she's very scared—like I was when my eyes stopped working and I went blind. And, maybe Earth's accident was caused by her moon, Luna, and Earth is scared her parents will blame Luna for the accident— like when I was afraid my parents were going to blame Moon for my accident," continued Erica.

"PLUS, maybe Earth can't take care of Luna the way she usually does, just like I can't take care of Moon because I am in the hospital. So, Earth might be afraid something is going to happen to Luna. I know I've been worrying that something might happen to Moon because I'm not there to take care of him.

"I also thought that maybe something already did happen to Luna. Maybe SHE got hit by a big rock, I mean an asteroid. And, maybe the asteroid caused some damage that astronomers haven't discovered yet."

"Erica, I am very impressed by your thoughtful reasoning AND your creative thinking!" stated Uncle Garwin. "I must say, it is absolutely brilliant that you have developed a theory based on all these similarities between you and Earth."

"It's my *EMPATHEORY!*" beamed Erica.

"*EMPATHEORY!* That's very creative! I like that! And I must say, I totally agree with you. I strongly believe that something very serious has happened to Earth, and we *do* need to find out what it is. It is also quite possible that Earth's secret may have something to do with Luna. Most certainly, life on Earth would change significantly if something happened to our moon. Hopefully we can find some more clues when I read the new transcripts to you," said Uncle Garwin."

"NEW TRANSCRIPTS? You mean there's *more*?"

"There will be!"

Uncle Garwin flipped open his cell phone and glanced at the flashing light.

"I left the SOS Receiver on *record*. Therefore, if the receiver registers any activity, it starts recording directly to my computer. Then the computer signals my cell phone with a beep, and a green light flashes while the SOS Receiver is recording. . . . I heard a beep while we were eating, so I checked to see if the green light was on," he said.

"WAS IT ON?"

"Well, yes, indeed. The green light was flashing then, and it is still flashing as we speak."

"This is SO EXCITING! When will I get to hear it?"

"I'll give you a chance to settle in and spend some time with Moon after you get home from the hospital tomorrow morning. Then I'll stop by in the afternoon and read the new transcripts to you," promised Uncle Garwin.

"I can't wait!" exclaimed Erica. "Tomorrow is going to be an ASTRONOMICAL day!"

The End
Of
BOOK ONE

The Author and Illustrator

Diane Janis was born in Philadelphia, Pa. She earned a Bachelor of Science Degree in Elementary Education and a Master's Degree in Education. Diane Janis was an elementary classroom teacher for fifteen years. Throughout her teaching career, she continually encouraged her students to use art and writing in all subject areas. She often incorporated her own creative writing, illustrations, and art projects into classroom activities. The *Earth's Secret*™ series originated from a short story that was created at home with her three children while she was working on a science lesson for her classroom.

Although she no longer teaches in the classroom, Diane Janis' teaching strategies continue on with her books and illustrations. Through her writing she tries to encourage children to increase their interest in science and environmental awareness, think creatively, develop a positive attitude, and overcome adversity.

Voices in the Dark was edited for factual content
by Dr. Ed Strother.

Dr. Ed Strother received his Ph.D. in experimental physics from the University of South Carolina. He has taught a wide range of courses in physics and the space sciences at the university level. As an astronomer and space scientist he has conducted a number of research projects sponsored by NASA and the USAF. Today, Dr. Strother consults on a wide range of scientific and educational projects and does technical editing and writing.